valiant

A Modern Tale of Faerie

HOLLY BLACK

simon pulse

NEW YORK   LONDON   TORONTO   SYDNEY

SIMON PULSE
An imprint of Simon & Schuster Children's Publishing Division
1230 Avenue of the Americas, New York, NY 10020
Copyright © 2005 by Holly Black
All rights reserved, including the right of reproduction in whole or in part in any form.
SIMON PULSE and colophon are registered trademarks of Simon & Schuster, Inc.
Also available in a Simon & Schuster Books for Young Readers hardcover edition.
Designed by Sammy Yuen Jr.
The text of this book was set in Meridien.
Manufactured in the United States of America
First Simon Pulse edition October 2006
8 10 9 7
The Library of Congress has cataloged the hardcover edition as follows:
Black, Holly.
Valiant: a modern tale of faerie / Holly Black.
p. cm.
Summary: Seventeen-year-old Val runs away to New York City, where she falls in with a gang of squatters who live in the city's subway system and consort with faeries, trolls, and other strange creatures.
ISBN-13: 978-0-689-86822-1 (hc.)
ISBN-10: 0-689-86822-7 (hc.)
[1. Supernatural—Fiction. 2. Magic—Fiction. 3. New York (N.Y.)—Fiction.]
[Fic]—22 2005298934
ISBN-13: 978-0-689-86823-8 (pbk.)
ISBN-10: 0-689-86823-5 (pbk.)

For my husband, Theo,
because he likes angsty, angry girls

Prologue

For I shall learn from flower and leaf
That color every drop they hold,
To change the lifeless wine of grief
To living gold.

—SARA TEASDALE, "ALCHEMY"

The tree woman choked on poison, the slow sap of her blood burning. Most of her leaves had already fallen, but those remaining blackened and shriveled along her back. She pulled her roots up from the deep soil, long hairy tendrils that flinched in the chill late autumn air.

An iron fence had surrounded her trunk for years, the stink of the metal as familiar as any small ache. The iron scorched her as she dragged her roots over it. She tumbled onto the concrete sidewalk, her slow tree thoughts filling with pain.

A human walking two little dogs stumbled against the brick wall of a building. A taxi screeched to a halt and blared its horn.

Long branches tipped over a bottle as the tree woman scrambled to pull away from the metal. She stared at the dark glass as it rolled into the street, watching the dregs of bitter poison drip out of the neck, seeing the familiar scrawl on the little strip of paper secured with wax. The contents of that bottle should have been a tonic, not the instrument of her death. She tried to lift herself up again.

One of the dogs started barking.

The tree woman felt the poison working inside of her, choking her breath and befuddling her. She had been crawling somewhere, but she could no longer remember where. Dark green patches, like bruises, bloomed along her trunk.

"Ravus," the tree woman whispered, the bark of her lips cracking. "Ravus."

holly black

Chapter 1

Now, here, you see, it takes all the running you can do,
to keep in the same place. If you want to get somewhere
else, you must run at least twice as fast as that!
    —LEWIS CARROLL, *THROUGH THE LOOKING GLASS*

Valerie Russell felt something cold touch the small of her back and spun around, striking without thinking. Her slap connected with flesh. A can of soda hit the concrete floor of the locker room and rolled, sticky brown liquid fizzing as it pooled. Other girls looked up from changing into sweats and started to giggle.

Hands raised in mock surrender, Ruth laughed. "Just a joke, Princess Badass of Badassia."

"Sorry," Val forced herself to say, but the sudden surprise of anger hadn't entirely dissipated and she felt like an idiot. "What are you doing down here? I thought being near sweat gave you hives."

Ruth sat down on a green bench, looking exotic in a vintage smoking jacket and long velvet skirt. Ruth's brows were thin pencil lines, her eyes outlined with black kohl and red shadow that made her look like a Kabuki dancer. Her hair was glossy black, paler at the roots and threaded with purple braids. She took a deep drag on her clove cigarette and blew smoke in the direction of one of Val's teammates. "Only my own sweat."

Val rolled her own eyes, but she smiled. She had to admit it was a fantastic response. Val and Ruth had been friends forever, for so long that Val was used to being the overshadowed one, the "normal" one, the one who set up the witty one-liners, not the one who delivered them. She liked that role; it made her feel safe. Robin to Ruth's Batman. Chewbacca to her Han Solo.

Val leaned down to kick off her sneakers and saw herself in the small mirror on her locker door, strands of orangy hair peeking out from a green bandanna.

Ruth had been dyeing her own hair since the fifth grade, first in colors you could buy in boxes at the supermarket, then in crazy, beautiful colors like mermaid green and poodle pink, but Val had only dyed her hair once. It had been a store-bought auburn; just darker and richer than her own pale color, but it had gotten her grounded anyway. Back then, her mother punished her every time she did anything to show that she was growing up. Mom didn't want her to get a bra, didn't want her to wear short skirts, and didn't want her dating until high school. Now that she was in high school, all of a sudden, her mother was pushing makeup and dating advice. Val had gotten used to pulling her hair back in bandannas, wearing jeans and T-shirts though, and didn't want to change.

"I've got some statistics for the flour-baby project and I picked out some potential names for him." Ruth unshouldered her giant messenger bag. The front flap was smeared with paint and studded with buttons and stickers—a pink triangle peeling at the edges, a button hand-lettered to say "Still Not King," a smaller one that read "Some things exist whether you believe in them or not," and a dozen more. "I was thinking maybe you could come over tonight and we could work on it."

"I can't," Val said. "Tom and I are going to see a hockey game in the city after practice."

"You're going to make a boy out of him yet," Ruth said, twirling one of her purple braids around her finger.

Val frowned. She couldn't help noticing the

edge in Ruth's voice when she talked about Tom. "Do you think he doesn't want to go?" Val asked. "Did he say something?"

Ruth shook her head and took another quick draw on her cigarette. "No. No. Nothing like that."

"I was thinking that we could go to the Village after the game if there's time. Walk around St. Mark's." Only a couple of months earlier, at the town fair, Tom had applied a press-on tattoo to the small of her back by kneeling down and licking the spot wet before pressing it to her skin. Now she could barely get him to have sex.

"The city at night. Romantic."

The way Ruth said it, Val thought she meant the opposite. "What? What's going on with you?"

"Nothing," Ruth said. "I'm just distracted or something." She fanned herself with one hand. "So many nearly naked girls in one place."

Val nodded, half-convinced.

"Did you look at those chat logs like I told you? Find that one where I sent you statistics about all-female households for the project?"

"I didn't get a chance. I'll find it tomorrow, okay?" Val rolled her eyes. "My mother is online twenty-four, seven. She has some new Internet boyfriend."

Ruth made a gagging sound.

holly black

"What?" Val said. "I thought you supported online love. Weren't you the one who said it was love of the mind? Truly spiritual without flesh to encumber it?"

"I hope I didn't say that." Ruth pressed the back of her hand to her forehead, letting her body tip backward in mock faint. She caught herself suddenly, jerking upright. "Hey, is that a rubber band around your ponytail? That's going to rip out your hair. Get over here; I think I have a scrunchie and a brush."

Val straddled the bench in front of Ruth and let her work out the band. "Ouch. You're making it worse."

"Aren't you athletic types supposed to be more butch?" Ruth brushed Val's hair out and threaded it through the cloth tie, pulling it tight enough so that Val thought she could feel the tiny hairs on the back of her neck snapping.

Jennifer walked up and leaned on her lacrosse stick. She was a plain, large-boned girl who'd been in Val's school since kindergarten. She always looked unnaturally clean, from her shiny hair to the sparkling white of her kneesocks and her unwrinkled shorts. She was also the captain of their team. "Hey lesbo, take it elsewhere."

"You afraid it's catching?" Ruth asked sweetly.

"Fuck off, Jen," Val said, less witty and a moment too late.

"You're not supposed to smoke here," said Jen, but she didn't look at Ruth. She stared at Val's sweats. Tom had decorated one side of them: drawing a gargoyle with permanent marker up a whole leg. The other side was mostly slogans or just random stuff Val had written with a bunch of different pens. They probably weren't what Jen thought of as regulation practicewear.

"Never mind. I got to go anyway." Ruth put out her cigarette on the bench, burning a crater in the wood. "Later, Val. Later, closet case."

"What is with you?" Jennifer asked softly, as though she really wanted Val to be her friend. "Why do you hang out with her? Can't you see what a freak she is?"

Val looked at the floor, hearing the things that Jen wasn't saying: *Are you a lesbian, too? Are you hot for me? We're only going to put up with you for so long on this team unless you shape up.*

If life were like a video game, she would have used her power move to whip Jen in the air and knock her against the wall with two strikes of a lacrosse stick. Of course, if life really were like a video game, Val would probably have to do that in a bikini and with giant breasts, each

8   holly black

one made of separately animated polygons.

In real real life, Val chewed on her lip and shrugged, but her hands curled into fists. She'd been in two fights already since she joined the team and she couldn't afford to be in a third one.

"What? You need your girlfriend to speak for you?"

Val punched Jen in the face.

Knuckles burning, Valerie dropped her backpack and lacrosse stick onto the already cluttered floor of her bedroom. Rummaging through her clothes, she snatched up underpants and a sports bra that made her even flatter than she already was. Then, grabbing a pair of black pants she thought were probably clean and her green hooded sweatshirt from the laundry pile, she padded out into the hall, cleated shoes scrunching fairy tale books free from their bindings and tracking dirt over an array of scattered video-game jewel cases. She heard the plastic crack under her heels and tried to kick a few to safety.

In the hall bathroom, she stripped off her uniform. After rubbing a washcloth under her arms and reapplying deodorant, she then started pulling on her clothes, stopping only to inspect the raw skin on her hands.

"This was your last shot," the coach had said. She'd waited three quarters of an hour in his office while everyone else practiced, and when he finally came in, she saw what he was going to say before he even opened his mouth. "We can't afford to keep you on the team. You are affecting everyone's sense of camaraderie. We have to be a single unit with one goal—winning. You understand, don't you?"

There was a single knock before her door opened. Her mother stood in the doorway, perfectly manicured hand still on the knob. "What did you do to your face?"

Val sucked her cut lip into her mouth, inspected it in the mirror. She'd forgotten about that. "Nothing. It was just an accident at practice."

"You look terrible." Her mother squeezed in, shaking out her recently highlighted blond bob so that they were both reflected in the same mirror. Every time she went to the hairdresser, he seemed to just add more and brighter highlights, so that the original brown seemed to be drowning in a rising tide of yellow.

"Thanks so fucking much." Val snorted, only slightly annoyed. "I'm late. Late. Late. Late. Like the white rabbit."

"Hold on." Val's mom turned and walked out

of the room. Val's gaze followed her down the hallway to the striped wallpaper and the family photographs. Her mother as a runner-up beauty queen. Valerie with braces sitting next to her mother on the couch. Grandma and Grandpa in front of their restaurant. Valerie again, this time holding her baby half sister at her dad's house. The smiles on their frozen faces looked cartoonish and their bared teeth were too white.

A few minutes later, Val's mother returned with a zebra-striped makeup bag. "Stay still."

Valerie scowled, looking up from lacing her favorite green Chucks. "I don't have time. Tom is going to be here any minute." She hadn't remembered to put on her own watch, so she pushed up the sleeve of her mother's blouse and looked at hers. He was already later than late.

"Tom knows how to let himself in." Valerie's mother smeared her finger in some thick, tan cream and started tapping it gently under Val's eyes.

"The cut is on my *lip*," Val said. She didn't like makeup. Whenever she laughed, her eyes teared and the makeup ran as if she'd been crying.

"You could use a little color in your face. People in New York dress up."

"It's just a hockey game, Mom, not the opera."

Her mother gave that sigh, the one that

seemed to imply that someday Val would find out just how wrong she was. She brushed Val's face with tinted powder and then with nontinted powder. Then there was more powder dusted on her eyes. Val recalled her junior prom last summer, and hoped her mother wasn't going to try and re-create that goopy, shimmery look. Finally, she actually painted some lipstick over Val's mouth. It made the wound sting.

"Are you done?" Val asked as her mom started on the mascara. A sideways look at her mother's watch showed that the train would leave in about fifteen minutes. "Shit! I have to go. Where the hell is he?"

"You know how Tom can be," her mother said.

"What do you *mean*?" She didn't know why her mother always had to act as if she knew Val's friends better than Val did.

"He's a boy." Val's mother shook her head. "Irresponsible."

Valerie fished out her cell from her backpack and scrolled to his name. It went right to voice mail. She clicked off. Walking back to her bedroom, she looked out the window, past the kids skateboarding off a plywood ramp in the neighbor's driveway. She didn't see Tom's lumbering Caprice Classic.

She phoned again. Voice mail.

"This is Tom. Bela Lugosi's dead but I'm not. Leave me a message."

"You shouldn't keep calling like that," her mother said, following her into the room. "When he turns his phone back on, he'll see how many calls he missed and who made them."

"I don't care what he sees," Val said, thumbing the buttons. "Anyway, this is the last time."

Val's mother shook her head and, stretching out on her daughter's bed, started to outline her own lips in brown pencil. She knew the shape of her own mouth so well that she didn't bother with a mirror.

"Tom," Valerie said into the phone once his voice mail picked up. "I'm walking over to the train station now. Don't bother picking me up. Meet me on the platform. If I don't see you, I'll take the train and find you at the Garden."

Her mother scowled. "I don't know that it's safe for you to go into the city by yourself."

"If we don't make this train, we're going to be late for the game."

"Well, at least take this lipstick." Val's mother rummaged in the bag and handed it over.

"How is that going to keep me safer?" Val muttered and slung her backpack over her shoulder.

Her phone was still clutched in her hand, plastic heating in her grip.

Val's mother smiled. "I have to show a house tonight. Do you have your keys?"

"Sure," Val said. She kissed her mother's cheek, inhaling perfume and hairspray. A burgundy lip print remained. "If Tom comes by, tell him I'm already gone. And tell him he's an asshole."

Her mother smiled, but there was something awkward about her expression. "Wait," she said. "You should wait for him."

"I can't," Val said. "I already told him I was going."

With that, she darted down the stairs, out the front door, and across the small patch of yard. It was a short walk to the station and the cold air felt good. Doing something other than waiting felt good.

The asphalt parking lot of the train station was still wet with yesterday's rain and the overcast sky swollen with the promise of more. As she crossed the lot, the signals started to flash and clang in warning. She made it to the platform just as the train ground to a stop, sending up a billow of hot, stinking air.

Valerie hesitated. What if Tom had forgotten his cell and waited for her at the house? If she left now and he took the next train, they might not find each other. She had both tickets. She might be able to leave his at the ticket booth, but he might not think to check there. And even if all that worked out, Tom would still be all broody. When or if he finally showed up, he wouldn't be in the mood to do anything but fight. She didn't know where they could go, but she'd hoped that they could find someplace to be alone for a little while.

She chewed the skin around her thumb, neatly biting off a hangnail and then pulling so a tiny strip of skin came loose. It was oddly satisfying, despite the tiny bit of blood that welled to the surface, but when she licked it away her skin tasted bitter.

The doors to the train finally shut, ending her indecision. Valerie watched as it rolled out of the station and then started walking slowly home. She was relieved and annoyed to spot Tom's car parked next to her mother's Miata in the driveway. Where had he been? She sped up and yanked open the door.

And froze. The screen slipped from her fingers, crashing closed. Through the mesh, she could see her mother bent forward on the white couch, crisp blue shirt unbuttoned past the top of her bra. Tom knelt on the floor, mohawked head leaning up to kiss her. His chipped black polished fingernails fumbled with the remaining buttons on her shirt. Both of them started at the sound of the door slamming and turned toward her, faces expressionless, Tom's mouth messy with lipstick. Somehow, Val's eyes drifted past them, to the dried-up daisies Tom had given her for their four-month anniversary. They sat on top of the television cabinet, where she'd left them weeks ago. Her mother had wanted Val to throw them out, but she'd forgotten. She could see the stems through the glass vase, the lower portion of them immersed in brackish water and blooming with mold.

Valerie's mother made a choking sound and fumbled to stand, tugging her shirt closed.

"Oh fuck," Tom said, half-falling onto the beige carpet.

Val wanted to say something scathing, something that would burn them both to ashes where they were, but no words came. She turned and walked away.

"Valerie!" her mother called, sounding more desperate than commanding. Looking back, she saw her mother in the doorway, Tom a shadow behind her. Valerie started to run, backpack banging against her hip. She only slowed when she was back at the train station. There, she squatted above the concrete sidewalk, ripping up wilted weeds as she dialed Ruth's number.

Ruth picked up the phone. She sounded as if she'd been laughing. "Hello?"

"It's me," Val said. She expected her voice to shake, but it came out flat, emotionless.

"Hey," Ruth said. "Where are you?"

Val could feel tears start to burn at the edges of her eyes, but the words still came out steady. "I found out something about Tom and my mother—"

"Shit!" Ruth interrupted.

Valerie went silent for a moment, dread making her limbs heavy. "Do you know something? Do you know what I'm talking about?"

"I'm so glad you found out," Ruth said, speaking fast, her words almost tripping over each other. "I wanted to tell you, but your mom begged me not to. She made me swear I wouldn't."

"She told you?" Val felt particularly stupid, but she just couldn't quite accept that she understood what was being said. "You knew?"

"She wouldn't talk about anything else once she found out that Tom let it slip." Ruth laughed and then stopped awkwardly. "Not like it's been going on for that long or anything. Honestly. I would have said something, but your mom promised she would do it. I even told her I was going to tell—but she said she'd deny it. And I did try to drop hints."

"What hints?" Val felt suddenly dizzy. She closed her eyes.

"Well, I said you should check the chat logs, remember? Look, never mind. I'm just glad she finally told you."

"She didn't tell me," Valerie said.

There was a long silence. She could hear Ruth breathing. "Please don't be mad," she said finally. "I just couldn't tell you. I couldn't be the one to tell you."

Val clicked off her phone. She kicked a stray chunk of asphalt into a puddle, and then kicked the puddle itself. Her reflection blurred; the only thing clearly visible was her mouth, a slash of red on a pale face. She smeared it, but the color only spread.

When the next train came, she got on it, sliding into a cracked orange seat and pressing her forehead against the cool plastiglass window. Her phone buzzed and she turned it off without looking at the screen. But as Val turned back toward the window, it was her mother's reflection she saw. It took her a moment to realize she was looking at herself in makeup. Furious, she walked quickly to the train bathroom.

holly black

The room was grubby and large, with a sticky rubber floor and hard plastic walls. The odor of urine mingled with the scent of chemical flowers. Small blobs of discarded gum decorated the walls.

Val sat down on the toilet lid and forced herself to relax, to take deep breaths of putrid air. Her fingernails dug into the flesh of her arms and somehow that made her feel a little better, a little more in control.

She was surprised by the force of her own anger. It overwhelmed her, making her afraid she might start screaming at the conductor, at every passenger on the train. She couldn't imagine lasting the whole trip. Already she was exhausted from the effort of keeping it together.

She rubbed her face and looked down at her palm, streaked with burgundy lipstick and shaking slightly. Val unzipped her backpack and poured its contents onto the filthy floor as the train lurched forward.

Her camera clattered on the rubber tile, along with a couple of rolls of film, a book from school—*Hamlet*—that she was supposed to have already read, a couple of hair ties, a crumpled package of gum, and a travel grooming case her mother had given her for her last birthday. She fumbled to open it—tweezers, manicuring scissors, and a razor, all glimmering in the dim light. Valerie took out the scissors, felt the small, sharp edges. She stood up and looked into the mirror. Grabbing a chunk of her hair, she started to chop.

Stray locks curved around her sneakers like copper snakes when she was done. Val ran a hand over her bald head. It was slick with pink squirt-soap and felt rough as a cat's tongue. She stared at her own reflection, rendered strange and plain, at unflinching eyes and a mouth pressed into a thin line. Specks of hair stuck to her cheeks like fine metal filings. For a moment, she couldn't be sure what that mirror face was thinking.

The razor and manicuring scissors clattered into the sink as the train lurched forward. Water sloshed in the toilet bowl.

"Hello?" someone called from outside the door. "What's going on in there?"

"Just a minute," Val called back. She rinsed off the razor under the tap and shoved it into her backpack. Slinging it over one shoulder, she got a wad of toilet paper, dampened it, and squatted down to mop up her hair.

The mirror caught her eye again as she straightened. This time, a young man looked back at her, his features so delicate that she didn't think he could defend himself. Val blinked, opened the

holly black

door, and stepped out into the corridor of the train.

She walked back to her seat, feeling the glances of the other passengers flinch from her as she passed. Staring out the window, she watched the suburban lawns slip by until they went into a tunnel and she saw only her new, alien reflection in the window.

The train pulled into an underground station and Val got off, walking through the stink of exhaust. She climbed up a narrow, unmoving escalator, crushed between people. Penn Station was thick with commuters, heads down as they passed one another and stands that sold pendants, scarves, and fiberoptic flowers that glowed with changing colors. Valerie stuck to one of the walls, passing a filthy man sleeping under a newspaper and a group of backpack-wearing girls screaming at one another in German.

The anger she had felt on the train had drained away and Val moved through the station like a sleepwalker.

Madison Square Garden was up another escalator, past a line of taxis and stands selling sugared peanuts and sausages. A man handed her a flyer and she tried to give it back, but he was already past her and she was left holding a sheet of paper promising "LIVE GIRLS." She crunched it up and stuffed it in her pocket.

She pushed through a narrow corridor jammed with people, and waited at the ticket counter. The young guy behind the glass looked up when she pushed Tom's ticket through. He seemed startled. She thought it might be her lack of hair.

"Can you give me my money back for that?" Val asked.

"You already have a ticket?" he asked, squinting at her as though trying to figure out exactly what her scam was.

"Yeah," she said. "My asshole ex-boyfriend couldn't make it."

Understanding spread across his features and he nodded. "Gotcha. Look, I can't give you your money back because the game's already started, but if you give me both I could upgrade you."

"Sure," Val said, and smiled for the first time that whole trip. Tom had already given her the money for his ticket and she was pleased that she could have the small revenge of getting a better seat from it.

He passed her the new ticket and she slid through the turnstile, wading her way through the crowd. People argued, faces flushed. The air stank of beer.

holly black

She'd been looking forward to seeing this game. The Rangers were having a great season. But even if they weren't, she loved the way the men moved on the ice, as though they were weightless, all the while balanced on knife blades. It made lacrosse look graceless, just a bunch of people lumbering over some grass. But as she looked for the doorway to her seat, she felt dread roiling in her stomach. The game mattered to all the other people the way it had once mattered to her, but now she was just killing time before she had to go home.

She found the doorway and stepped through. Most of the seats were already occupied and she had to sidle past a group of ruddy-faced guys. They craned their necks to look around her, past the glass divider, to where the game had already started. The stadium *smelled* cold, the way the air did after a snowstorm. But even as her team skated toward a goal, her thoughts flickered back to her mother and Tom. She shouldn't have left the way she had. She wished she could do it over. She wouldn't even have bothered with her mother. She would have punched Tom in the face. And then, looking just at him, she would have said, "I expected as much from her, but I would have thought better of you." That would have been perfect.

Or maybe she could have smashed the windows of his car. But the car was really a piece of junk, so maybe not.

She could have gone over to Tom's house though, and told his parents about the dime bag of weed he kept between his mattress and box spring. Between that and this thing with Val's mother, maybe his family would have sent him off to some detention facility for mom-fucking, drug-addict freaks.

As for her mother, the best revenge Val could ever have would be to call her dad, get her stepmother, Linda, on speakerphone, and tell them the whole thing. Val's dad and Linda had a perfect marriage, the kind that came with two adorable, drooling kids and wall-to-wall carpeting and mostly made Val sick. But telling them would make the story theirs. They would tell it whenever they wanted, shout it at Val's mother when they fought, report it to shock their golfing buddies. It was Val's story and she was going to control it.

There was a roar from the audience. All around her, people jumped to their feet. One of the Rangers had thrown some guy from the other team down and was ripping off his own gloves. The referee grabbed hold of the Ranger, and his

holly black

skate slid, slicing a line across the other player's cheek. As they were cleared away, Val stared at the blood on the ice. A man in white came and scraped up most of it and the Zamboni smoothed the ice during halftime, but a patch of red remained, as though the stain had soaked so deep it couldn't be drawn out. Even as her team made the final winning goal and everyone near her surged to their feet again, Val couldn't seem to look away from the blood.

After the game, Val followed the crowd out onto the street. The train station was only a few steps away, but she couldn't face going home. She wanted to delay a little longer, until she could figure things out, dissect what had happened a little more. The very idea of getting back on the train filled her with a sick panic that made her pulse race and her stomach churn.

She started to walk and, after a while, she noticed that the street numbers got smaller and the buildings got older, lanes narrowed and the traffic thinned out. Turning left, toward what she thought might be the edge of the West Village, she passed closed clothing stores and rows of parked cars. She wasn't quite sure of the time, but it had to be nearly midnight.

Her mind kept unraveling the looks between

Tom and her mother, glances that now had meaning, hints she should have picked up on. She saw her mother's face, some weird combination of guilt and honesty, when she'd told Val to wait for Tom. The memory made Val flinch, as though her body were trying to throw off a physical weight.

She stopped and got a slice of pizza at a sleepy shop where a woman with a shopping cart full of bottles sat in the back, drinking Sprite through a straw and singing to herself. The hot cheese burned the roof of Val's mouth, and when she looked up at the clock, she realized she'd already missed the last train home.

Chapter 2

Trying their wings once more in hopeless flight:
Blind moths against the wires of window screens.
Anything. Anything for a fix of light.
—X. J. KENNEDY, "STREET MOTHS," THE LORDS OF MISRULE

Val dozed off again, her head pillowed on an almost-empty backpack, the rest of her spread across the cold floor tiles under the subway map. She'd picked out a place to nap near the token booth, figuring no one would try to rob her or stab her right in front of people.

She had spent most of the night in the hazy state between sleep and wakefulness, nodding off for a moment, then jolting awake. Sometimes she'd woken from a dream and not known where she was. The station stank of rancid trash and mold, even without the heat to make scents bloom. Above the cracked paint and mildew, a sculptural border of curling tulips was a remnant of another Spring Street station, one that must have been old and grand. She tried to imagine that station as she slipped back to sleep.

The strangest thing was that she wasn't scared. She felt removed from everything, a sleepwalker who had stepped off the path of normal life and into the forest where anything could happen. Her anger and hurt had cooled into a lethargy that left her limbs heavy as lead.

The next time she blearily opened her eyes, people stood over her. She sat up, the fingers on one hand digging into her backpack, the other hand coming up as if to ward off a blow. Two cops stared down at her.

"Morning," one of them said. He had short gray hair and a ruddy face, as if he'd been standing too long in the wind.

"Yeah." Val wiped jagged bits of sleep from the corners of her eyes with the heel of her hand. Her head hurt.

"This is a pretty shitty crash spot," he said. Commuters passed them, but only a few bothered to look her way.

Val narrowed her eyes. "So?"

"How old are you?" asked his partner. He was younger, slim, with dark eyes and breath that smelled like cigarettes.

holly black

"Nineteen," Val lied.

"Got any I.D.?"

"No," Val said, hoping that they wouldn't search her backpack. She had a permit, no license since she had failed her driving test, but the card was enough to prove she was only seventeen.

He sighed. "You can't sleep here. You want us to bring you someplace you can get a little rest?"

Val stood up, slinging her pack over one shoulder. "I'm fine. I was just waiting for morning."

"Where are you going?" the older cop asked, blocking her way with his body.

"Home," Val said because she thought that would sound good. She ducked under his arm and darted up the steps. Her heart hammered as she raced up Crosby Street, through the crowds of people, past the groggy early-morning workers dragging around their backpacks and briefcases, past the bike messengers and taxis, stepping through the gusts of steam that billowed up from the grates. She slowed and looked back, but no one seemed to be following her. As she crossed to Bleecker, she saw a couple of punks drawing on the sidewalk with chalk. One had a rainbow mohawk, slightly dented at the top. Val stepped around their art carefully and kept going.

For Val, New York was always the place that

made Val's mother hold her hand tight, the glittering grid of glass-paned skyscrapers, the steaming Cup O' Noodles threatening to pour boiling broth on kids waiting in line for TRL just blocks away from where *Les Misérables* played to matinees of high school French students bused in from the suburbs. But now, crossing onto Macdougal, New York seemed so much more and less than her idea of it. She passed restaurants sleepily stirring with activity, their doors still shut; a chain-link fence decorated with more than a dozen locks, each one decoupaged with a baby's face; and a shop that sold only robot toys. Small, interesting places that suggested the vastness of the city and the strangeness of its inhabitants.

She ducked into a dimly lit coffeehouse called Café Diablo. The inside was wallpapered in red velvet. A wooden devil stood by the counter, holding out a silver tray nailed to his hand. Val bought a large coffee, nearly choking it with cinnamon, sugar, and cream. The heat of the cup felt good against her cold fingers, but it made her aware of the stiffness of her limbs, the knots in her back. She stretched, arching up and twisting her neck until she heard something pop.

She headed for a spot in the back, picking a

threadbare armchair near a table where a boy with tiny dreads and a girl with tangles of faded blue hair and knee-high white boots whispered together. The boy ripped and poured sugar packet after sugar packet into his cup.

The girl moved slightly and Val could see that she had a butterscotch kitten on her lap. It stretched one paw to bat at the zipper on the girl's patchy rabbit-fur coat.

Val smiled reflexively. The girl saw her looking, grinned back, and put the cat on the table. It mewed pitifully, sniffed the air, stumbled.

"Hold on," Val said. Popping off the lid of her coffee, she went up to the front, filled it with cream, and set it down in front of the cat.

"Brilliant," the blue-haired girl said. Val could see that her nose stud was infected, the skin around the glittering stone swollen tight and red.

"What's its name?" Val asked.

"No name yet. We've been discussing it. If you have any ideas let me know. Dave doesn't think we should keep her."

Val took a swig of her coffee. She couldn't think of anything. Her brain felt swollen, pressing against her skull, and she was so tired that her eyes didn't focus right away when she blinked. "Where'd she come from? Is she a stray?"

The girl opened her mouth, but the boy put his hand on her arm. "Lolli." He squeezed warningly, and the two shared an intense glance.

"I stole her," Lolli said.

"Why do you tell people things like that?" Dave asked.

"I tell people everything. People only believe what they can handle. That's how I know who to trust."

"You shoplifted her?" Val asked, looking at the kitten's tiny body, the curling pink tongue.

Lolli shook her head, clearly delighted with herself. "I threw a rock through the window. At night."

"Why?" Val slipped easily into the role of appreciative audience, making the right noises, like she did with Ruth or Tom or her mother, asking the questions the speaker wanted asked, but under that familiar habit was real fascination. Lolli was exactly what Ruth wanted to be with all her posturing.

"The woman who owned the pet store smoked. Right in the store. Can you believe that? She didn't deserve to take care of animals."

"You smoke." Dave shook his head.

"I don't own a pet shop." Lolli turned to Val. "Your head looks cool. Can I touch it?"

holly black

Val shrugged and bent her head forward. It felt strange to be touched there—not uncomfortable, just weird, as though someone were stroking the soles of her feet.

"I'm Lollipop," the girl said. She turned to the boy with the dreads. He was thin and pretty looking, with Asian eyes. "This is Sketchy Dave."

"Just Dave," Dave said.

"I'm just Val." Val sat up. It was a relief to talk to people after so many hours of silence. It was even more of a relief to talk to people who didn't know anything about her, Tom, her mother, or any of her past.

"Not short for Valentine?" Lollipop asked, still smiling. Val wasn't sure if the girl was making fun of her or not, but since her name was *Lollipop*, how funny could Val's name be? She just shook her head.

Dave snorted and ripped open another sugar packet, pouring the grains onto the table and cutting them into long lines that he ate with a coffee-wetted finger.

"Do you go to school around here?" Val asked.

"We don't go to school anymore, but we live here. We live wherever we want to."

Val took another sip of coffee. "What do you mean?"

"She doesn't mean anything," Dave interrupted. "How about you?"

"Jersey." Val looked at the milky gray liquid in her cup. Sugar crunched between her teeth. "I guess. If I go back." She got up, feeling stupid, wondering if they were making fun of her. "'Scuse me."

Val went to the bathroom and washed up, which made her feel less disgusting. She gargled tap water, but when she spat, she saw herself in the mirror too clearly: splotches of freckles across her cheeks and mouth, including one just below her left eye, all of them looking like ground-in dirt against the patchy tan she had from outdoor sports. Her newly shaved head looked weirdly pale and the skin around her blue eyes was bloodshot and puffy. She scrubbed her hand over her face, but it didn't help. When she came back out, Lolli and Dave were gone.

Val finished her coffee. She thought about napping in the armchair, but the café had grown crowded and loud, making her headache worse. She walked out to the street.

A drag queen with a beehive wig hanging at a lopsided angle chased a cab, one Lucite shoe in her hand. As the cabbie sped away, she threw it hard enough that it banged into his rear window.

"Fucking fucker!" she screamed as she limped toward her shoe.

Val darted out into the street, picked it up, and returned it to its owner.

"Thanks, lambchop."

Up close, Val could see her fake eyelashes were threaded with silver, and glitter sparkled along her cheekbone.

"You make a darling prince. Nice hair. Why don't we pretend I'm Cinderella and you can put that shoe right on my foot?"

"Um, okay," Val said, squatting down and buckling the plastic strap, while the drag queen tried not to hop as she swayed to keep her balance.

"Perfect, doll." She righted her wig.

As Val stood up, she saw Sketchy Dave laughing as he sat on the metal railing on the other side of the narrow street. Lolli was stretched out on one side of a batiked blue sheet that held books, candleholders, and clothing. In the sunlight, the blue of Lolli's hair glowed brighter than the sky. The kitten was stretched out beside her, one paw batting a cigarette over the ground.

"Hey, *Prince Valiant*," Dave called, grinning like they were old friends. Lolli waved. Val shoved her hands in her pockets and walked over to them.

"Pop a squat," Lolli said. "I thought we scared you off."

"Headed somewhere?" Dave asked.

"Not really." Val sat down on the cold concrete. The coffee had finally started racing through her veins and she felt almost awake. "What about you?"

"Selling off some stuff Dave scrounged. Hang out with us. We'll make some money and then we'll party."

"Okay." Val wasn't sure she wanted to party, but she didn't mind sitting on the sidewalk for a while. She picked up the sleeve of a red velvet jacket. "Where did all this stuff come from?"

"Dumpster-diving mostly," Dave said, unsmiling. Val wondered if she looked surprised. She wanted to seem cool and unfazed. "You'd be amazed what people will pay for what they throw out in the first place."

"I believe it," Val said. "I was thinking how nice that jacket is."

That must have been the right response, because Dave grinned widely, showing a chipped front tooth. "You're okay," he said. "So, what, you said 'if you go back'? What's that about? You on the street?"

Val patted the concrete. "I am right now."

holly black

They both laughed at that. As Val sat beside them, people passed by her, but they only saw a girl with dirty jeans and a shaved head. Anyone from school could have walked past her, Tom could have stopped to buy a necktie, her mother could have tripped on a crack in the sidewalk, and none of them would have recognized her.

Looking back, Val knew she had a habit of trusting too much, being too passive, too willing to believe the best of others and the worst of herself. And yet, here she was, falling in with more people, getting swept along with them.

But there was something different about what she was doing now, something that filled her with a strange pleasure. It was like looking down from a high building, the way the adrenaline hit you as you swayed forward. It was powerful and terrible and utterly new.

Val spent the day there with Lolli and Dave, sitting on the sidewalk, talking about nothing. Dave told them a story about a guy he knew who got so drunk that he ate a cockroach on a dare. "One of those New York cockroaches, ones that are the size of goldfish. The thing was halfway out of his mouth and still squirming as he bit down on it. Finally, after chewing and chewing he actually swallows. And my brother is there—Luis is some kind of crazy smart, like he read the encyclopedia when he was home with chicken pox smart—and he says, 'You know that roaches lay eggs even after they're dead.' Well, this guy can't believe it, but then he starts yelling how we are trying to kill him and holding his stomach, saying he can already feel them eating him from the inside."

"That is nasty," Val said, but she was laughing so hard she had tears in her eyes. "So deeply nasty."

"No, but it gets better," said Lolli.

"Yeah," Sketchy Dave said. "Because he pukes on his shoes. And the roach is right there, all chopped up, but clearly pieces of a big black bug. And here's the thing—one of the legs moves."

Val shrieked with disgust and told them about the time that she and Ruth smoked catnip thinking it would get them high.

When they had sold a faux crocodile-skin clutch, two T-shirts, and a sequined jacket from the blanket, Dave bought them all hot dogs off a street cart, fished out of the dirty water and slathered with sauerkraut, relish, and mustard.

"Come on. We need to celebrate finding you," Lolli said, jumping to her feet. "You and the cat."

Still eating, Lolli jogged down the street. They crossed over several blocks, Lolli in the lead, until they came to an old guy rolling his own cigarettes on the steps of an apartment building. A filthy bag filled with other bags sat beside him. His arms were as thin as sticks and his face was as wrinkled as a raisin, but he kissed Lolli on the cheek and said hello to Val very politely. Lolli gave him a couple of cigarettes and a crumpled wad of bills, and he stood up and crossed the street.

"What's wrong with him?" Val whispered to Dave. "Why's he so skinny?"

"Just cracked out," Dave said.

A few minutes later, he came back with a bottle of cherry brandy in a brown paper bag.

Dave rummaged up an almost-empty cola bottle from his messenger bag and filled that with the liquor. "So the cops don't stop us," he said. "I hate cops."

Val took a swig from the bottle and felt the alcohol burn all the way down her throat. The three of them passed it back and forth as they walked down West Third. Lolli stopped in front of a table covered in beaded earrings hanging from plastic trees that jangled whenever a car went past. She fingered a bracelet made with tiny silver bells. Val walked to the next table, where incense was stacked in bundles and samples burned on an abalone tray.

"What have we here?" asked the man behind

the counter. He had skin the color of polished mahogany and smelled of sandalwood.

Val smiled mildly and turned back toward Lolli.

"Tell your friends to take more care whom they serve." The incense man's eyes were dark and glittered like a lizard's. "It's always the messengers who are the first to know the customer's displeasure."

"Right," Val said, stepping away from the table. Lolli skipped up, bells jangling around her wrist. Dave was trying to make the cat lick brandy out of the soda cap.

"That guy was really weird," Val said. When she looked back, out of the corner of her eye, for just a moment, the incense man seemed to have long spines jutting up from his back like a hedgehog.

Val reached for the bottle.

They walked aimlessly until they came to a triangle-shaped median of asphalt, lined on both sides with park benches, presumably for suits to eat their lunch in warmer weather and suck in the humid air and car exhaust. They sat, letting the cat down to investigate the flattened remains of a pigeon. There, they passed the brandy back and forth until Val's tongue felt numb and her teeth tingled and her head swam.

holly black

"Do you believe in ghosts?" Lolli asked.

Val thought about that for a moment. "I guess I'd like to."

"What about other things?" Lolli mewed, rubbing her fingers together to call the cat over. It paid no attention.

Val laughed. "What things? I mean, I don't believe in vampires or werewolves or zombies or anything like that."

"What about faeries?"

"Faeries like . . . ?"

Dave chuckled. "Like monsters."

"No," Val said, shaking her head. "I don't think so."

"Want to know a secret?" Lolli asked.

Val leaned in close and nodded. Of course she did.

"We know where there's a tunnel with a monster in it," Lolli half-whispered. "A faerie. We know where the faeries live."

"What?" Val wasn't sure she'd heard Lolli right.

"Lolli," Dave warned, but his voice sounded a little slurred, "shut up. Luis would be raging if he heard you."

"You can't tell me what to say." Lolli wrapped her arms around herself, digging her nails into her skin. She tossed back her hair. "Who would believe her anyway? I bet she doesn't even believe me."

"Are you guys serious?" Val asked. Drunk as she was, it almost seemed possible. Val tried to think back to the fairy tales she liked to re-read, the ones she'd collected since she was a little kid. There weren't very many faeries in them. At least not what she thought of as faeries. There were godmothers, ogres, trolls, and little men that bargained their services for children, then railed at the discovery of their true names. She thought of faeries in video games, but they were elves, and she wasn't sure if elves were faeries at all.

"Tell her," Lolli said to Dave.

"So how come you get to order me around?" Dave asked, but Lolli just punched him in the arm and laughed.

"Fine. Fine." Dave nodded. "My brother and I used to do some urban exploring. You know what that is?"

"Breaking into places you're not supposed to be," Val said. She had a cousin who went out to Weird NJ sites and posted photos of them on his Web site. "Mostly old places, right? Like abandoned buildings?"

"Yeah. There're all kinds of things in this city that most people can't see," Dave said.

"Right," said Val. "White alligators. Mole people. Anacondas."

Lolli got up and retrieved the cat from where it was scratching at the dead bird. She held it on her lap and petted it hard. "I thought that you could handle it."

"How come you know about this stuff that no one else does?" Val was trying to be polite.

"Because Luis has the second sight," Lolli said. "He can see them."

"Can *you* see them?" Val asked Dave.

"Only when they let me." He looked at Lolli for a long moment. "I'm freezing."

"Come back with us," Lolli said, turning to Val.

"Luis won't like it." Dave turned his boot as if he were squashing a bug.

"We like her. That's all that matters."

"Where are we going back to?" Val asked. She shivered. Even though she was warm from the liquor drowsing through her veins, her breath gusted in the air and her hands alternated between icy and hot when she pressed them under her shirt and against her skin.

"You'll see," said Lolli.

They walked for a while and then ducked down into a subway station. Lollipop stepped through the turnstile with a swipe of her card, then passed it back through the bars to Dave. She looked at Val. "Coming?"

Val nodded.

"Stand in front of me," Dave said, waiting.

She walked up to the turnstile. He swiped, then pressed himself against her, pushing them both through at once. His body was corded muscle against her back and she smelled smoke and unwashed clothes. Val laughed and staggered a little.

"I'll tell you something else you don't know," Lolli said, holding up several cards. "These are toothpick MetroCards. You break off toothpicks real little and then you jam them in the machine. People pay, but they don't get their cards. It's like a lobster trap. You come back later and see what you caught."

"Oh," Val said, her head swimming with brandy and confusion. She wasn't sure what was true and what wasn't.

Lollipop and Sketchy Dave walked to the far end of the subway platform, but instead of stopping at the end and waiting for the train, Dave jumped down into the well where the tracks ran. A few people waiting for the train glanced over and then quickly looked away, but most of them didn't even seem to notice. Lolli followed Dave awkwardly, moving so that she was sitting on the edge and then letting him half lift her down. She held on to the now-squirming kitten.

"Where are you going?" Val asked, but they were already disappearing into the dark. As Val jumped down onto the litter-strewn concrete after them, she thought how insane it was to follow two people she didn't know into the bowels of the subway, but instead of being afraid, she felt glad. She would make all her own decisions now, even if they were ruinous ones. It was the same pleasurable feeling as tearing a piece of paper into tiny, tiny pieces.

"Be careful not to touch the third rail or you'll fry," Dave's voice called from somewhere ahead.

Third rail? She looked down nervously. The middle one. It had to be the middle one. "What if a train comes?" Val asked.

"See those niches?" Lolli called. "Just flatten yourself into one of those."

Val looked back at the concrete of the subway platform, much too high to climb. Ahead, there was darkness, studded only with tiny lamps that seemed to give off little real light. Rustling noises seemed too close, and she thought she felt tiny paws run over one sneaker. She felt the panic she had been waiting for this whole time. It swallowed her up. She stopped, so gripped by fear that she couldn't move.

"Let's go." Lolli's voice came from the gloom. "Keep up."

Val heard the distant rattle of a train but couldn't tell how far away it was or even what track it was on. She ran to catch up to Lolli and Dave. She had never been afraid of the dark, but this was different. The darkness here was devouring, thick. It seemed like a living thing, breathing through its own pipes, heaving gusts of stench into the tunnel around her.

The smell of filth and wetness was oppressive. Her ears strained for the steps of the other two. She kept her eyes on the lights, as though they were a breadcrumb trail, leading her out of danger.

A train rushed by on the other side of the tracks, the sudden brightness and furious noise stunning her. She felt the pull of the air, as though everything in the tunnels was being drawn toward it. If it had been on her side, she would have never had time to jump for the niche.

"Here." The voice was close, surprisingly close. She couldn't be sure whether it belonged to Lolli or to Dave.

Val realized she was standing next to a platform. It looked like the station they'd left, except

holly black

here the tiled walls were covered in graffiti. Mattresses were piled on the concrete shelf, heaped with blankets, throw pillows, and couch cushions—most of them in some variation of mustard yellow. Candle stubs flickered dimly, some jammed in the sharp mouths of beer cans, others in tall glass jars decorated with the Virgin Mary's face on the label. A boy with his hair braided thickly back from his face sat near a hibachi grill in the back corner of the station. One of his eyes was clouded over, whitish and strange, and steel piercings puckered his dark skin. His ears were bright with rings, some thick as worms, and a bar stuck out from either cheek, as though to highlight his cheekbones. His nose was pierced through one nostril and a hoop threaded his lower lip. As he stood, Val saw that he wore a puffy black jacket over baggy and ripped jeans. Sketchy Dave started up a make-shift ladder of wood planking.

Val turned all the way around. One of the walls was decorated with spray paint that read "for never and ever."

"She's impressed," Lolli said. Her voice echoed in the tunnel.

Dave snorted and walked over to the fire. He took out flattened cigarette butts from his messenger bag and dropped them into one of the chipped mugs, then stacked cans of peaches and coffee.

The boy with the piercings lit up one of the butts and took a deep drag. "Who the fuck is that?"

"Val," Val said before Lolli could answer. Val shifted her weight, uncomfortably aware that she didn't know the way back.

"She's my new friend," Lollipop said, settling down in a nest of blankets.

The pierced boy scowled. "What's with her hair? She some kind of cancer patient?"

"I cut it," Val said. For some reason that made both the pierced boy and Sketchy Dave laugh. Lolli looked pleased with her.

"If you didn't guess, this is Luis," Lolli said.

"Don't enough people find their own way down here without you two playing tour guide?" Luis demanded, but no one answered him, so perhaps his question was merely talking.

Exhaustion was starting to creep over Val. She settled down on a mattress and pulled a blanket over her head. Lolli was saying something, but the combination of brandy, ebbing fear, and exhaustion was overwhelming. She could always go home later, tomorrow, in a few days. Whenever. As long as it wasn't now.

As she dozed off, Lolli's cat climbed over her, jumping at shadows. She reached out her hand to it, sinking her fingers into the short, soft fur. It was a tiny thing, really, but already crazy.

Chapter 3

I have found the warm caves in the woods,
filled them with skillets, carvings, shelves,
closets, silks, innumerable goods;
fixed the suppers for the worms and the elves.
—Anne Sexton, "Her Kind"

Muscles clenching, Val vaulted out of sleep into being fully awake, her heart beating hard against her chest. She nearly cried out before she remembered where she was. She guessed it was afternoon, although it was still dark in the tunnels; the only light came from the guttering candles. On the other mattress, Lollipop was curled up with her back against Luis. He had one arm thrown over her. Sketchy Dave was on her other side, swaddled up in a dirty blanket, head bent toward Lolli the way the branch of a tree grows toward the sun.

Val buried her head deeper in the comforter, even though it smelled vaguely of cat piss. She felt groggy but better rested.

holly black

Lying there, she remembered looking through college catalogues a couple of weeks earlier with Tom. He'd been talking about Kansas, which had a good writing program and wasn't crazy expensive. "And look," he'd said, "they have a girls' lacrosse team," as if maybe they'd be together after high school. She'd smiled and kissed him while she was still smiling. She'd liked kissing him; he always seemed to know just how to kiss back. Thinking about it made her feel aching and dumb and betrayed.

She wanted to go back to sleep but she couldn't, so she just stayed still until she had to pee badly enough to go and squat, wide-legged, over the stinking bucket she found in one corner. She tugged down her jeans and underwear, trying to balance on the balls of her feet, while she pulled the crotch of her clothes as far away from her body as she could. She tried to tell herself that it was the same as when you were driving down a highway and there was no rest stop, so you had to go in the woods. There was no toilet paper and no leaves, so she did a little hopping dance that she hoped would shake herself dry.

Making her way back, she saw Sketchy Dave starting to stir and hoped that she hadn't woken him up. She tucked her legs back into the blanket, now noticing that the vivid odors of the platform combined into a smell she couldn't identify. Light streamed down from a grate in the street above, illuminating black, grime-streaked iron beams.

"Hey, you slept for almost fourteen hours," he said, turning on his side and stretching. He was shirtless, and even in the gloom she could see what looked like a bullet wound in the center of his chest. It pulled the rest of his skin toward it, a sinking pool that drew everything to his heart.

Dave moved over to the hibachi and kindled it with matches and balls of newspaper. Then he set a pot on top, shaking grounds out of a tin and pouring water from a plastic gallon milk jug.

She must have stared at him for too long, because he looked up with a grin. "Want some? It's cowboy coffee. No milk, but there's plenty of sugar if you want it."

Nodding, she bundled the blankets around her. He strained her a steaming cup and she held it gratefully, using it first to warm her hands and then her cheeks. She ran her fingers absently over her scalp. She felt thin stubble, like fine sandpaper.

"You might as well come scrounging with me," Sketchy Dave said, looking over at the mattress

holly black

with something like longing. "Luis and Lolli'll sleep forever if you let 'em."

"How come you're up?" she asked, and took a sip from the mug. The coffee was bitter, but Val found it satisfying to drink, flavored with smoke and nothing else. Grounds floated on the surface, making a black film.

He shrugged. "I'm the junkman. Gotta go see what the suits throw out."

She nodded.

"It's a skill, like those pigs that can smell out truffles. You either got it or you don't. One time I found a Rolex watch in with some junk mail and burned toast. It was like someone tossed everything on the kitchen table right into the garbage without looking at it."

Despite what Dave had said about them sleeping in, Lolli groaned and slid out from under Luis's arm. Her eyes were still mostly closed and she had a dirty kimono-style dressing gown thrown over yesterday's clothes. She looked beautiful in a way that Val never would, lush and hard all at the same time.

Lolli gave Luis a shove. He grunted and rolled over, propping himself up on his elbows. There was a flicker of movement along the wall and the cat strolled out, butting its head against Luis's hand.

"She likes you, see?" Lolli said.

"Aren't you worried about rats getting her?" Val asked. "She's kind of little."

"Not really," Luis said darkly.

"Come on, you just named her last night." Lolli picked the cat up and dumped her on her own lap.

"Yeah," Dave said. "Polly and Lolli."

"Polyhymnia," said Luis.

Val leaned forward. "What does Poly-whatever mean?"

Dave poured another cup for Luis. "Polyhymnia's some kind of Greek Muse. I don't know which one. Ask him."

"Doesn't matter," Luis said, lighting a cigarette stub.

Sketchy Dave shrugged, as if apologizing for knowing as much as he did. "Our mom used to be a librarian."

Val didn't really know what a Muse was, except for a dim recollection of studying the *Odyssey* in ninth grade. "What's your mom now?"

"Dead," said Luis. "Our dad shot her."

Val caught her breath and was about to stammer out an apology, but Sketchy Dave spoke first.

"I thought maybe I'd be a librarian, too." Dave looked at Luis. "The library is a good place to

holly black

think. Kind of like down here." He turned back to Val. "Did you know I was the first one to find this spot?"

Val shook her head.

"Scrounged it. I'm the prince of refuse, the lord of litter."

Lolli laughed and Dave's smile broadened. He seemed more pleased by his joke now that he knew Lolli liked it.

"You didn't want to be a librarian," Luis said, shaking his head.

"Luis knows all about mythology." Lolli took a sip of coffee. "Like Hermes. Tell her about Hermes."

"He's a psychopomp." Luis gave Val a dark look, as if daring her to ask what that meant. "He travels between the world of the living and the world of the dead. A courier, kind of. That's what Lolli wants me to say. But forget that for a minute; you asked about rats getting Polly. What do you know about rats?"

Val shook her head. "Not much. I think one stepped over my foot on my way in here."

Lolli snorted and even Dave smiled, but Luis's face was intense. His voice had a ritual quality, as though he'd said this many times before. "Rats get poisoned, shot, trapped, beaten, just like street people, just like *people*, just like us. Everybody hates rats. People hate the way they move, the way they hop, they hate the sound of their paws skittering all over the floor. Rats're always the villains."

Val looked into the shadows. Luis seemed to be waiting for her to react, but she didn't know what the right response was. She wasn't even sure she knew what he was really talking about.

He went on. "But they're strong. They got teeth that are tougher than iron. They can gnaw through anything—wood beams, plaster walls, copper pipes—anything but steel."

"Or diamond," Lolli said with a smirk. She didn't seem at all unnerved by his speech.

Luis barely paused to acknowledge Lolli had spoken. His eyes stayed on Val. "People used to fight them in pits here in the city. Fight them against ferrets, against dogs, against people. That's how tough they are."

Dave smiled, as if all this made sense to him.

"They're smart, too. You ever see a rat on the subway? Sometimes they get on a car at one platform and detrain at the next stop. They're taking a ride."

"I've never seen that," Lolli scoffed.

"I don't care if you ever saw it or not." Luis looked at Dave, who'd stopped nodding. Then he

holly black

turned to Val. "I can sing rats' praises morning, noon, and night and it won't change the way you feel about them, will it? But what if I told you that there were things out there that think of you like you think of rats?"

"What things?" Val asked, remembering what Lolli had said the night before. "Do you mean fa—"

Lolli sunk her nails into Val's arm.

Luis looked at her for a long time. "Another thing about rats. They're *neophobic*. You know what that means?"

Val shook her head.

"They don't trust new things," said Luis, unsmiling. "And neither should we." Then he got up, chucking his stub of a cigarette out onto the tracks, and walked up the steps and out of the station.

What an asshole. Val picked at a loose thread on her pants, pulling at it, unraveling the fabric. *I should go home,* she thought. But she didn't go anywhere.

"Don't worry about him," Lolli said. "Just because he can see things we can't, he thinks he's better than us." She watched until Luis was out of sight and then picked up a small lunchbox with a pink cat on it. Opening the latch, she took out and unrolled a T-shirt to spread out the contents: a syringe, an antique silver-plated spoon with some of the silver worn off, a pair of flesh-toned pantyhose, several tiny press-and-seal baggies containing an amber powder that glimmered a faint blue in the dim light. Lolli shouldered off one sleeve of her dressing gown and Val could see black marks on the inside of her elbow, like the skin there was charred.

"Chill out, Lolli," Sketchy Dave said. "Not in front of her. Not this."

Lolli reclined against a pile of pillows and bags. "I like needles. I like the feeling of the steel under my skin." She looked at Val. "You can get a little buzz off shooting up water. You can even shoot up vodka. Goes right into your bloodstream. Makes you drunker cheaper."

Val rubbed her arm. "It can't be too much worse than you scratching me." She should have been horrified, but the ritual of it fascinated her, the way all the tools were laid out on the dirty shirt, waiting to be used in turn. It made her think of something, but she wasn't quite sure what.

"I'm sorry about your arm! He was in such a mood, I didn't want him to get started about the faeries." Lolli made a face as she cooked the powder with a little water over the hibachi. It bubbled on the spoon. The sweet smell, like burnt sugar, filled Val's nose. Lolli sucked it up through the

holly black

needle, then tapped the bubbles to the top, pushing them out with a squirt of liquid. Tying off her upper arm with pantyhose, Lolli inserted the tip slowly into one of the black marks on her arm.

"Now I'm a magician," Lolli said.

It came to Val then that what she was reminded of was her mother putting on makeup—laying out the tools and then using them one by one. First foundation, then powder, eye shadow, eyeliner, blush, all done with the same calm ceremony. The fusion of the images unnerved her.

"You shouldn't do that in front of her," Dave repeated, signaling in Val's direction with a bob of his chin.

"She doesn't mind. Do you, Val?"

Val didn't know what she thought. She'd never seen anyone give themselves a shot like that, professional as a doctor.

"She's not supposed to see," Dave said. Val watched him get up to pace the platform. He stopped under a mosaic of tiles spelling out "WORTH." Behind him, she thought she saw the darkness change its shape, spreading like ink dropped into water. Dave seemed to see it, too. His eyes widened. "Don't do this, Lolli."

The gloom seemed to be coalescing into indistinct shapes that made the hair stand up on Val's arms. Blurry horns, mouths crowded with teeth, and claws as long as branches formed and then dissipated.

"What's the matter? You scared?" Lolli sneered at Dave before turning back to Val. "He's afraid of his own shadow. That's why we call him Sketchy."

Val said nothing, still staring at the moving darkness.

"Come on," Dave said to Val, moving unsteadily toward the stairs. "Let's go scrounge."

Lolli pouted exaggeratedly. "No way. I found her. She's my new friend and I want her to stay here and play with me."

Play with her? Val didn't know what Lolli meant, but she didn't like the sound of it. Right then, Val wanted nothing more than to get out of the claustrophobic tunnels and away from the shifting shade. Her heart beat so fast that she feared it would spring out of her chest like the bird in a cuckoo clock. "I have to get some air." She stood up.

"Stay," Lolli said lazily. Her hair seemed bluer than it had a moment ago, shot through with aquamarine highlights, and the air flickered around her the way it did over a street in the hot sun. "You won't believe how much fun you'll have."

holly black

"Let's go," Dave said.

"Why do you always have to be so boring?" Lolli rolled her eyes and lit her cigarette off of the fire. A good half of it went up in flames, and she dragged on it anyway. Her voice was slow, slurred, but her gaze, even from drowsy eyes, was severe.

Dave started up the yellow maintenance stairs and Val followed him quickly, filled with an uncertain dread. At the top, Dave pushed up the grating and they stepped out onto the sidewalk. As she emerged into the bright, late-afternoon sunlight, she realized that she'd left her backpack on the platform with her return ticket still inside of it. She half-turned back to the grate and then hesitated. She wanted the bag, but Lolli had been acting so strange . . . everything had gone so strange. But maybe even the smell of the drug could make shadows move? She ran through a health-class list of substances to avoid—heroin, PCP, angel dust, cocaine, crystal meth, special K. She didn't know much about any of them. No one she knew did anything more than smoke weed or drink.

"Coming?" Dave called. She noticed the worn-down soles of his boots, the stains covering his jeans, the tightly corded muscles of his thin arms.

"I left my—," she started to say, but then thought better of it. "Never mind."

"It's just the way Lolli is," he said with a sad smile, looking at the sidewalk and not at Val's eyes. "Nothing's going to change her."

Val looked around at the large building across the street and the concrete park they were standing in, with its dried-up and cracked pond, and an abandoned shopping cart. "If it's so easy to get in this way, why did we come through the tunnels?"

Dave looked uncomfortable and he was silent for a moment. "Well, the financial district is pretty packed around five on a Friday, but it's nearly empty on a Saturday. You don't want to be coming up out of the sidewalk with a million people around."

"Is that all?" Val asked.

"And I didn't trust you," Dave said.

Val tried to smile, because she guessed that he had a little faith in her now, but all she could think of was what would have happened if somewhere, walking through the tunnels, he had decided that he couldn't trust her.

Val picked through a Dumpster. The food smells still made her gag, but after two previous trash piles, she was getting more used to them. She pushed aside mounds of shredded paper, but found only a few boards studded with nails, empty

holly black

CD cases, and a broken picture frame.

"Hey, look at this!" Sketchy Dave called from the next bin. He emerged wearing a navy pea coat, one arm of it slightly ripped, and holding up a Styrofoam take-out box that looked like it was mostly filled with linguini in alfredo sauce. "You want some?" he asked, picking up a hunk of noodles and dropping them into his mouth.

She shook her head, disgusted but laughing.

Pedestrians were wending their way home from work, messenger bags and briefcases slung across their shoulders. None of them seemed to see Val or Dave. It was as if the two of them had become invisible, just part of the trash they were sorting through. It was the sort of thing that she'd heard about on television and in books. It was supposed to make you feel small, but she felt liberated. No one was looking at her or judging her based on whether her outfit matched or who her friends were. They didn't see her at all.

"Isn't it too late to find anything good?" Val asked, hopping down.

"Yeah, morning is the best time. Around now on the weekday, businesses are junking office stuff. We'll see what's around, then come back out near midnight, when restaurants toss off the day-old bread and vegetables. And then at dawn you go residential again—we'll have to get there before the trucks pick up."

"You can't do this every day, though, right?" She looked at him incredulously.

"It's always trash day somewhere."

She glanced at a stack of magazines tied together with string. So far, she hadn't found anything she thought was worth taking. "What exactly are we looking for?"

Dave ate the last of the linguini and tossed the box back into a Dumpster. "Take any porn. We can always sell that. And anything nice, I guess. If you think it's nice, someone else probably will, too."

"How about that?" She pointed to a rusted iron headboard leaning against an alley wall.

"Well," he said, as if trying to be kind, "we could truck it up to one of those fancy little shops—they paint old stuff like this and resell it for big money—but they wouldn't pay enough for the trouble it'd be." He looked at the dimming light in the sky. "Shit. I have to pick something up before it gets dark. I might have to do a delivery."

Val picked up the headboard. The rust scraped off on her hands, but she managed to balance the cast iron on her shoulder. Dave was right. It was heavy. She put it back down again. "What kind of delivery?"

"Hey, look at this," Dave squatted down and yanked out a box full of romance novels. "These might be something."

"To who?"

"We could probably sell 'em," he said.

"Yeah?" Val's mother had read romances and she was used to the sight of the covers: a woman tipped back in a man's arms, her hair long and flowing, a beautiful house in the distance. All the fonts curled and some were embossed with gold. She bet none of these books had to do with fucking your daughter's boyfriend. She wanted to see one of the covers show that—a young kid and an old lady with too much makeup and lines around her mouth. "Why would anyone want to read that shit?"

Dave shrugged, carried the box under one arm, and flipped open a book. He didn't read out loud, but his mouth moved as he scanned the page.

They were quiet as they walked for a while and then Val pointed to the book in his hand. "What's it about?"

"I don't know yet," Sketchy Dave said. He sounded annoyed. They walked for a while more in silence, his face buried in the book.

"Look at that," Val pointed to a wooden chair with the seat gone.

Dave regarded it critically. "Nah. We can't sell

that. Unless you want it for yourself."

"What would I do with it?" Val asked.

Dave shrugged and turned to walk through a black gate into a mostly empty square, dumping the romance novel back into the box. Val stopped to read the plaque: Seward Park. Tall trees shadowed most of the deserted playground equipment sprawled over the space. The concrete was carpeted with yellow and brown leaves. They passed a dried-up fountain with stone seals that looked as if they might spurt water for kids to run through in the summertime. The statue of a wolf peeked out from a patch of brown grass.

Sketchy Dave walked past all that without pausing and headed for a separate gated area that bordered one of the New York Public Library branches. Dave slid through a gap in the fence. Val followed, climbing into a miniature Japanese garden filled with small piles of smooth, black rocks in stacks of varying heights.

"Wait here," he said.

He pushed over one of the stone piles and lifted up a small, folded note. Moments later he was back out through the fence and unfolding it.

"What does it say?" Val asked.

With a grin, Dave held the paper out. It was blank.

holly black

"Watch this," he said. Crumpling it into a ball, he threw it into the air. It flew out onto the path and downward, when it suddenly changed direction as though blown by a rebel wind. As Val watched in amazement, the paper ball rolled until it rested beneath the base of a slide.

"How did you do that?" Val asked.

Dave reached underneath the slide and ripped a tape-covered object free. "Just don't tell Luis, okay?"

"Do you say that about everything?" Val looked at the object in Dave's hand. It was a beer bottle, corked with melted wax. Around the neck, a scrap of paper hung from a ragged piece of string. Inside, molasses-brown sand sifted with each tilt of the container, showing a purplish sheen. "What's the big deal?"

"Look, if you don't believe Lolli, I'm not going to argue with you. She told you too much already. But just say that you did believe Lolli for a minute, and say you thought that Luis could see a whole world the rest of us can't, and say that he does some jobs for them."

"Them?" Val couldn't decide if she thought this was a conspiracy to freak her out or not.

Dave squatted down, and with a quick look at the sun's position in the sky, uncorked the bottle, causing the wax around the neck to crumble. He sifted a little of the contents into a tiny baggie like the one she'd seen Lolli pour her drug out of. He shoved the baggie into the front pocket of his jeans.

"Come on, what is it?" Val asked, but her voice was hushed now.

"I can honestly say I have no fucking clue," Sketchy Dave said. "Look. I have to go uptown and drop this off. You can come along with me, but you have to hang back when we get there."

"Is that the stuff Lolli shot in her arm?" Val asked.

Dave hesitated.

"Look," Val said. "I can just ask Lolli."

"You can't believe everything Lolli says."

"What is that supposed to mean?" Val demanded.

"Nothing." Dave shook his head and walked off. Val had no choice but to follow him. She wasn't even sure she could find her way back to the abandoned platform without him to guide her and she needed her bag to go anywhere else.

They took the F to Thirty-fourth Street, then switched to the B, taking that all the way to Ninety-sixth. Sketchy Dave held on to a horizontal metal bar and did pull-ups as the train thundered through the tunnels.

holly black

Val looked out the train window, watching the small lights marking distance streak by, but after a while her eyes were drawn to the other passengers. A wiry black man with close-cropped hair swayed unconsciously to the music on his iPod, a load of manuscripts balanced in one arm. A girl seated next to him was carefully drawing a glove of inky swirls up her own hand. Leaning against the doors, a tall man in a striped gray suit clutched his briefcase and stared at Dave in horror. Each person seemed to have a destination, but Val was a piece of driftwood, spinning down a river, not even sure in what direction she was moving. But she knew how to make herself spin faster.

From the station, they walked a few blocks to the edge of Riverside Park, a sprawling patch of green that sloped down the highway to the water beyond. Across the street, town houses with park views had curling ironwork at the windows and doors. Intricately carved concrete blocks framed doorways and stair railings, forming fantastical dragons and lions and griffons that leered down at her in the reflected glow of street lamps. Val and Dave passed a fountain where a stone eagle with a cracked beak glowered over a murky green pool choked with leaves.

"Just wait here," Sketchy Dave said.

"Why?" Val asked. "What is the big deal? You already told me all kinds of shit you aren't supposed to."

"I told you you're not supposed to be along."

"Fine." Val relented and sat down on the edge of the fountain. "I'll be right here."

"Good," Dave said and jogged across the street to a door without iron grillwork. He walked up the white steps, put down the box of romance novels, and pressed a buzzer near where someone had stenciled a mushroom with spray paint. Val glanced up at the sculpted gargoyles that flanked the roof of the building. As she was looking, one seemed to shudder, like a bird on a perch, stony feathers rustling and then settling. Val froze, staring at it, and after a moment, the gargoyle went still.

Val jumped up and crossed the street, calling Dave's name. But as she got to the steps, the black door opened and a woman stepped into the doorway. She wore a long white slip. Her tangled, brown-and-green hair looked unwashed and the skin under her eyes was dark as a bruise. Hooves peeked out from under the hem of the slip where feet should have been.

Val froze, and the skirt settled, covering them, leaving Val unsure of what she'd seen.

Sketchy Dave turned his head and gave Val a

fierce glare before he took out the beer bottle from his bag.

"Come inside?" the hoofed woman asked, her voice rough, as though she'd been shouting. She didn't seem to notice that the seal had been broken.

"Yeah," Sketchy Dave said.

"Who's your friend?"

"Val," Val said, trying not to gape. "I'm new. Dave's showing me the ropes."

"She can wait out here," said Dave.

"Do you think me so discourteous? The chill air will cut her to the bone." The woman held open the door and Val followed Dave inside, smirking. There was a marble-lined hall and a staircase railed with old, polished wood. The hooved woman led them through sparsely furnished rooms, past a fountain where silvery koi darted, their bodies so pale that the pink of their insides showed through their scales, past a music room holding only a double-strung lap harp on a table of marble, then into a parlor. She sat down on a cream-colored settee, the brocade fabric worn thin, and beckoned for them to join her. There was a low table near her and on it a glass, a teapot, and a tarnished spoon. The hooved woman used the spoon to measure out some of the amber sand into her cup, then filled it with hot water and drank deeply. She flinched once and when she looked up, her eyes shone with an eerie, glittering brightness.

Val couldn't stop her gaze from straying to the woman's goat feet. There was something obscene about the glimpses of short, thick fur that covered her slender ankles, the sheen of the black horn, the two splayed toes.

"Sometimes a remedy can seem another sort of sickness," the goat-footed woman said. "David, be sure to tell Ravus there's been another murder."

Sketchy Dave sat down on the ebonized wood floor. "Murder?"

"Dunnie Berry died last night. Poor thing, she was just coming out of her tree—it's horrible how that iron gate fences her roots. It must have scorched her every time she crossed it. You delivered to her, no?"

Sketchy Dave shifted uncomfortably. "Last week. Wednesday."

"You might well be the last person to have seen her alive," the goat-footed woman said. "Be careful." She lifted her teacup, swigged down a bit more of the solution. "People are saying your master peddles poison."

"He's not my master." Sketchy Dave stood up. "We've got to go."

The goat-footed woman stood, too. "Of course.

holly black

Come in the back and I'll get what I owe."

"Don't eat or drink anything or you'll be more fucked than you already are," Dave whispered to Val as he followed the woman into another room, leaving his salvaged box of romance novels on the floor. Val scowled and walked over to a display case. Inside the glass door was a large, solid chunk of something like obsidian. Beside it were some other things, equally odd. A bit of bark, a broken stick, a sharp burr in the shape of a pinecone, each fold razor sharp.

A few moments later, Sketchy Dave and the goat-footed woman returned. She was smiling. Val tried to stare at her without catching her eye. If someone had asked Val what she would do if she saw some supernatural creature, she wouldn't have figured she'd do nothing at all. She felt unable to be sure of what she was seeing, unable to decide if there really was a monster right in front of her. As they walked out of the apartment, Val could hear her blood thundering in her head to the speeding beat of her heart.

"I told you to fucking stay over there," Sketchy Dave growled, gesturing across the street, toward the fountain.

Val was too flustered to be angry. "I saw something—a statue—moving." She pointed upward, to the top of the building and the almost-night sky but she was incoherent. "And then I came over and . . . what is she?"

"Fuck!" Dave punched the stone wall, his knuckles coming away raw and scraped. "Fuck! *Fuck!*" He walked away, head hunched as though he were leaning into a strong wind.

Val caught up to him and grabbed him by the arm. "Tell me," she demanded, her grip tightening. He tried to jerk away from her, but he couldn't. She was stronger.

He looked at her strangely, like he was reevaluating them both. "You didn't see anything. There was nothing to see."

Val stared at him. "And what would Lolli say? A faerie, right? Except faeries don't fucking exist!"

He started to laugh. She dropped his arm and shoved him hard. The box of novels fell, scattering paperbacks into the road.

He looked down at them and then back at her. "Fucking bitch," he said and spat on the ground.

All the rage and bewilderment of the last day boiled up in her. Her hands balled into fists. She wanted to hit something.

Dave bent down to pick up the cardboard box and replaced the fallen books. "You're lucky you're a girl," he muttered.

holly black

Chapter 4

We must not look at goblin men,
We must not buy their fruits:
Who knows upon what soil they fed
Their hungry thirsty roots?

—CHRISTINA ROSSETTI, "GOBLIN MARKET"

On the train ride back, Val sat in a plastic seat far from Dave, leaned her head against a Plexiglas-covered map of the subway, and wondered how a person could have hooves. She'd seen shadows move on their own and bottles of brown sand that had something to do with make-believe gossip about murdered tree people from weird, Upper West Side ladies. What she did know was that she didn't want to be blind and dumb, the kind of girl that didn't notice that her mom and boyfriend were having sex until she saw it with her own eyes. She wanted to know the truth.

When Val got close to the concrete park on Leonard Street she saw Luis sitting on a ledge, drinking something out of a blue glass bottle. A bird-boned girl with mismatched sneakers and a swollen belly sat beside him, trembling fingers holding a cigarette. As Val got closer, she could see sores on the new girl's ankles, leaking pus. The streets were nearly deserted, the only person close by a security guard across the street who walked out to the curb every now and then before she disappeared into the building.

"Why are you still around?" Luis asked, glancing up at her. She was unnerved by the stare from his cloudy eye.

"Just tell me where Lolli is and I won't be," said Val.

Luis gestured with his chin to the grate in the ground as Dave walked up to them both.

The girl dropped her cigarette and then reached for it, her fingers grazing the hot end without her seeming to notice as she fumbled to put it back in her mouth.

"What did you do?" Luis asked Dave, his jaw tightening. "What happened?"

Dave looked at the parked cars that lined the street. "It wasn't my fault."

Luis closed his eyes. "You are such a fucking idiot."

Dave said something else, but Val had already

holly black

started walking toward the service entrance, the grate that she and Dave had slid out of that afternoon. She got down on her hands and knees, pulled up the unhinged end of the metal bars, and lowered herself onto the steps.

"Lolli?" she called into the darkness.

"Over here," came the drowsy reply.

Val waded across the mattresses and blankets to where she'd slept the night before. Her backpack wasn't where she'd left it. She kicked aside some of the dirty clothes on the platform. Nothing. "Where's my bag?"

"You trust a bunch of bums with your stuff, I guess you get what you get." Lolli laughed and held up the knapsack. "It's here. Chill."

Val unzipped her pack. All her stuff was inside, the razor still choked with her hair, the thirteen dollars still folded up in her wallet right beside her train ticket. Even her gum was still there. "Sorry," Val said and sat down.

"Don't trust us?" Lolli grinned.

"Look, I saw something and I don't know what it was and I'm done getting fucked with."

Lolli sat up, hugging her legs to her chest, eyes wide and smile stretching even wider. "You saw one of them!"

The image of the goat-footed woman moved

uneasily behind Val's eyes. "I know what you're going to say, but I don't think it was a faerie."

"So what do you think it was?"

"I don't know. Maybe my eyes were playing tricks on me." Val sat down on an overturned wood tangelo box. It made a cracking sound, but supported her weight. "That doesn't make any sense."

"Believe what you can handle believing."

"But, I mean—faeries? Like 'clap if you believe in faeries'?"

Lolli snorted. "You saw one. You tell me."

"I did tell you. I told you I don't know what I saw. A woman with goat feet? You shooting something weird in your arm? Paper that dances around? Is that supposed to add up?"

Lolli scowled.

"How do you *know* it's real?" Val demanded.

"The troll tunnel," Lolli said. "You won't be able to explain that away."

"Troll?"

"Luis made a deal with him. It was when Dave and their mom got shot. Their mother was dead when the ambulance came, but Dave was in the hospital for a while. Luis promised the troll he would serve him for a year if he saved Dave's life."

holly black

"That's who Dave was doing the delivery for?" Val asked.

"He took you on one of those?" Lolli blew out a breath that might have been a laugh. "Wow, he really is the worst spy in the world."

"What is the big deal about telling me? Why does Luis care what I know? Like you said to Dave, no one is going to believe me."

"Luis says none of us are supposed to know, not even Dave. *They*'d be mad, he says. But since he started doing deliveries for Ravus, some of the other faeries have him doing errands for them. Dave does some of the troll's jobs."

"My friend Ruth used to make up things. She said she had a boyfriend named Zachary who lived in England. She showed me letters full of angsty poetry. Basically, the truth was that Ruth wrote herself letters, printed them out, and lied about it. I know all about liars," Val said. "It's not like I don't believe what you're saying, but what if Luis is lying to you?"

"What if he is?" asked Lolli.

Val felt a burst of anger, the worse because it was directionless. "Whatever. Where's the troll tunnel? We'll find out for ourselves."

"I know the way," Lolli said. "I followed Luis to the entrance."

"But you didn't go inside?" Val stood up.

"No." Lolli stood, too, dusting off her skirt. "I didn't want to go alone and Dave wouldn't come with me."

"What do you think a troll is?" Val asked as Lolli scrounged through the cloth and bags on the platform. Val thought of the story of the three goats, thought of the game *WarCraft* and the little green trolls that carried axes and said, "Wanna buy a cigar?" and "Say hello to my little friend" when you clicked on them enough times. None of that seemed real, but the world would certainly be cooler with something so unreal in it.

"Got it," Lolli said, holding up a flashlight that gave off a dim and inconstant glow. "This isn't going to last."

Val jumped off onto the track level. "We'll be quick."

With a sigh, Lolli climbed down after her.

As they walked through the subway tunnel, the failing flashlight washed the black walls amber, highlighting the soot and the miles of electrical cording that threaded through the tunnel. It was like moving through the veins of the city.

They passed a live platform, where people waited for a train. Lolli waved to them as they stared, but Val reached down and picked up the

holly black

discarded batteries of a dozen CD players. As they moved on, she tried each battery in turn, until she found two that strengthened the beam of the flashlight.

Now it lit piles of garbage, catching the green reflection of rat eyes and the moving walls of roaches that throve in the heat and the dark. Val heard a thin whistle.

"Train," Val yelled, pushing Lolli against the gap in the wall, a shallow crevice thick with grime. Dust gusted through the air a moment before the train barreled past on another track. Lolli cackled and pressed her face close to Val's.

"One fine day in the middle of the night," she intoned. "Two dead boys got up to fight."

"Stop it," Val said, pulling away.

"Back to back they faced each other, pulled out their swords and shot one another. The deaf cop on the beat heard the noise and came and shot the two dead boys." Lolli laughed. "What? It's a rhyme my mother used to tell me. You never heard it before?"

"It's creepy as shit."

Val's knees were shaky as they resumed walking through the endless twisting tunnels. Finally, Lolli pointed to an opening that looked as if it had been bashed through the cement blocks. "Through there," she said.

Val took a step, but Lolli made a noise. "Val," she started, but she didn't continue.

"If you're scared, you can wait here. I'll go in and come right back out."

"I'm not *scared*," Lolli said.

"Okay." Val stepped through the rough concrete doorway.

There was a corridor, murky with water, with calcium deposits hanging down in brittle, chalky stalactites. She took a few more steps, cold water soaking her sneakers and the hem of her jeans. The light from the flashlight lit torn, ragged strips of plastic sheeting directly ahead of her. They shifted with the slight wind, like gauzy draperies or ghosts. The movement was unnerving. Splashing along, she ducked through the plastic and into a large chamber choked with roots. They dangled everywhere, long feathery tendrils dragging in the deeper water, thick root trunks cracking through the concrete ceiling to thin and spread. But the strangest part was that fruit hung from them as from branches. Pale globes grew from the hairy coils, warmed by no sun and fed by no soil. Val walked closer. The skin of each was milky and translucent, showing a rose blush beneath it, as though their centers might be red.

Lolli touched one. "They're warm," she said.

holly black

It was then that Val noticed rusted stairs, their railing wrapped with sodden cloth.

She hesitated at the bottom of them. Glancing at the inverted tree again, she tried to tell herself that it was just weird, not supernatural. It didn't matter. It was too late to turn back.

Val started up the steps. Each one echoed and she could see a diffuse light. As trains rumbled above them, a thin, powdery dust fell like rain, catching and streaking the weeping walls. The girls spiraled up, higher and higher until they came to a large casement window shrouded by old blankets hung with nails. Val leaned over the railing and pushed aside the cloth. She was surprised to see a basketball court, apartment buildings, the highway, and the river beyond, sparkling like a necklace of lights. She was inside the Manhattan Bridge.

She kept walking, finally coming to a large open room with pipes and thick cords running along the ceiling and heavy wooden ladders along both sides of the wall. It looked as if it was meant for maintenance workers. Books were piled up on the makeshift shelves and in dusty stacks on the floor. Old volumes, tattered and worn. A sheet of plywood rested atop several dozen cinderblocks near the doorway, creating a makeshift desk. Jam jars lined one edge, and resting against it was a sword that looked as though it was made of glass.

Val took a step closer, reaching out her hand, when something fell on her. It was cold and formless, like a heavy wet blanket, and it stretched to cover her. It blocked out her sight and choked her. She threw up her hands, clawing at the slightly damp stuff, feeling it give under her sharp, short nails. Dimly, she could hear Lolli shrieking as if from very far away. Spots started to form in front of Val's eyes and she reached blindly for the sword. Her hand slid over the blade, cutting her fingers shallowly, but letting her blindly find the hilt.

She braced and swung at her own shoulder. The thing slipped from her, and for a dizzying moment she could breathe again. Hefting the sword of glass as much as she could like a lacrosse stick, she chopped at the white, boneless thing that rippled toward her, its stretched face and flat features making it appear like a pallid, fleshy paper doll. It writhed on the ground and went limp.

Val's hands shook. She tried to still them, but they wouldn't stop trembling, even when she clenched them into fists and dug her fingernails into the heels of her hands.

"What was that thing?" Lolli asked.

holly black

Val shook her head. "How the fuck would I know?"

"We should be quick." Lolli walked over to the desk and dumped several jars into her bag.

"What are you doing?" Val asked. "Let's get out of here."

"Okay, okay," Lolli said, rummaging through some bottles. "I'm coming."

Herbs were bound into bundles in one of the jam jars. Another was full of dead wasps, but a third was filled with what looked like knots of red licorice shoelaces. Some had labels on their lids: chokecherry, hyssop, wormwood, poppy. At the center of the plywood was a marble cutting board with spiky green balls waiting to be chopped by the tin half-moon of a knife that rested beside them.

On the wall were a series of pinned objects—a candy wrapper, a gray wad of chewing gum, the burned-out stub of a cigarette. Hanging in front of each was a magnifying glass, enlarging not only the items but also the handwritten notes surrounding each. "Breath," read one. "Love," read another.

Lolli gasped sharply. Val spun around without thinking, lifting the sword automatically. Someone loomed in the doorway, tall and lean as a basketball player, bending to duck under the doorframe. As he straightened up, lank hair, black as ink, framed the grayish-green skin of his face. Two undershot canines jutted from his jaw, their tips sinking into the soft flesh of his upper lip. His eyes went wide with something that might have been fear or even fury, but she found herself transfixed by the way the black irises were dusted around the edges with gold, like the eyes of a frog.

"Well." The troll's voice was a deep growl. "What have we here? A pair of filthy street girls." He took two steps toward Val and she stumbled backward, tripping over her own feet, her mind filled only with panic.

With one booted foot, the troll nudged the boneless thing. "I see you've gotten past my guardian. How unlikely." He wore a buttoned black coat that covered him from neck to calf, with black trousers underneath that seemed to emphasize the shock of green at the frayed cuffs and nape where cloth met flesh. His skin was the same horrible color that you might find underneath a band of copper you'd worn for too long. "And you've helped yourself to something else of mine as well."

Fear closed up Val's throat and held her in place. She watched the milky blood run down the sword and felt her hands start to shake again.

holly black

"There is only one human who knows this place. So what did Luis tell you?" The troll took another step toward them, his voice soft and furious. "Did he dare you to go inside? Did he say there was a *monster*?"

Val looked at Lolli, but she was stunned and silent.

The troll ran the point of his tongue over an incisor. "But what did Luis intend, that's the real question. To give you a good scare? To give *me* a good scare? A good *meal*? It is entirely possible Luis might think I would want to eat you." He paused, as if waiting for one of them to deny it. "Do you think I want to eat you?"

Val raised the blade of the sword.

"*Really*? You don't say?" But then his voice deepened to a bellow. "Of course, perhaps you are merely a pair of unlucky *thieves*."

Val's instincts took over. She ran toward the exit, toward the troll. As he reached for her, she ducked, passing under his arm and hitting the strips of plastic. She was halfway down the stairs when she heard Lolli scream.

Standing there, trains rattling on the bridge overhead, still holding the glass sword, she hesitated. *She* was the reason Lolli was inside this place. It was Val's own dumb idea to try to prove to herself that faeries were real. She should have gone back when she saw the tree. She shouldn't have come here at all. Taking a deep breath, she ran back up the stairs.

Lolli was sprawled out on the ground, tears running down her face, her body gone weirdly lax. The troll held her by the wrist and seemed to be in the middle of demanding something from her.

"Let her go," Val said. Her voice sounded like someone else's. Someone brave.

"I think not." Leaning down, he ripped Lolli's messenger bag off her shoulder and tipped it upside down. Several coins bounced on the wood floor, rolling next to bottles filled with black sand, needles, a rusted knife, sticks of gum, cigarette butts, and a compact that cracked as it hit the wood, spilling powder across the floor. He reached down for one of the bottles, long fingers nearly touching the neck. "Why would you want—"

"We don't have anything else of yours." Val stepped forward and raised the blade. "Please."

"Really?" He snorted. "Then what have you got in your hands?"

Val looked at the sword, gleaming like an icicle under the fluorescent lights, and was surprised. She'd forgotten that it was his. Turning the point

holly black

toward the floor, she considered dropping it, but was afraid to be wholly unarmed. "Take it. Take it and we'll go."

"You are in no position to command me," said the troll. "Put down the sword. Carefully. It is a thing more precious than you."

Val hesitated, bending as if she was going to set down the glass blade. Not placing it on the ground, she still watched him.

He twisted Lolli's finger abruptly and she shrieked. "May it pain her each time she itches to reach for a thing that isn't hers." He grasped a second finger. "And may it pain you to think you're the cause of her pain."

"Stop!" Val shouted, dropping the sword onto the wood planks of the floor. "I'll stay if you let her go."

"What?" His eyes narrowed, then one black eyebrow rose. "Aren't you the gallant?"

"She's my friend," Val said.

He paused and his face went curiously blank. "Your friend?" he repeated tonelessly. "Very well. You will pay for her foolishness as well as your own. That is the burden of friendship."

Val must have looked relieved, because a small, cruel smile crept onto his face. "How much time is she worth? A month of service? A year?" Lolli's eyes sparkled with tears.

Val nodded. Sure. Anything. Whatever. Just let them leave and then it wouldn't matter what she'd promised.

He sighed. "You will serve me for a month, one week for each item stolen." Pausing for a moment, he added, "In whatever way that I need."

She flinched and he smiled.

"Each dusk you will go to Seward Park. There, you will find a note under the wolf's paw. If you do not do what it says, things will go hard with you. Do you understand?"

Val nodded. He dropped Lolli's hand. She scrambled to shove her things back into her bag.

The troll pointed with one long finger. "Go over to that table. On it, there is a tincture, marked 'Straw.' Bring it to me."

Val fumbled with the jars, reading the looping handwriting: toadflax, knotweed, rue, bloodroot, mugwort. She held up a solution, its contents thick and cloudy.

He nodded. "Yes, that. Bring it here."

She did so, walking close to him, close enough to notice that the cloth of his coat was wool, tattered and full of moth holes. Small, curved horns grew through the top of each ear, making the tips seem like they were hardening to bone.

He took the jar, opened it, and scooped up

holly black

some of the contents. She flinched away from him; the solution smelled like rotten leaves.

"Stay," he said, as though she were a dog brought to heel.

Angry at her own terror but hopeless against it, she remained motionless. He ran the pads of his fingers over her mouth, slicking them with the stuff. She had braced herself for his skin to feel oily or horrible, but it was merely warm.

Then, when he looked into her face, his gaze was so intent that she shuddered. "Repeat the conditions of your promise."

She did.

People said that video games were bad because they made you numb to death, made you register entrails spattering across a screen as a sign of success. In that moment, Val thought that the real problem with games was that the player was supposed to try everything. If there was a cave, you went in it. If there was a mysterious stranger, you talked to him. If there was a map, you followed it. But in games, you had a hundred million billion lives and Val only had this one.

Chapter 5

Nothing farther then he uttered—not a feather then he
  fluttered—
Till I scarcely more than muttered, "Other friends have
  flown before—
On the morrow he will leave me, as my Hopes have
  flown before."
Then the bird said, "Nevermore."

—EDGAR ALLAN POE, "THE RAVEN"

The city lights were bright and the streets were
clogged with smokers standing outside of bars and
restaurants when Val and Lolli staggered out of the
bridge and onto the street.

A man sleeping on broken-down cardboard
rolled over and wrapped an overcoat tighter
around himself. Val started violently at the movement, her muscles clenching so fast that her shoulders hurt. Lolli cradled her messenger bag as if it
were a stuffed animal, wrapping her arms around
it and herself.

It was strange how when crazy things happened, it was hard to follow the tracery of reasons

holly black

and impulses and thoughts that got you to the crazy place. Even though Val had wanted to find evidence of faeries, the actual proof was over-whelming. How many faeries were there and what other things might there be? In a world where faeries were real, might there be demons or vampires or sea monsters? How could these things exist and it not be on the front cover of every newspaper everywhere?

Val remembered her father reading *The Three Billy Goats Gruff* when she was a little kid. *Trip trap, trip trap went the littlest Billy Goat Gruff.* This troll was nothing like the illustration in the book—were any of them? *Who's that tripping over my bridge?*

"Look at my finger," Lolli said, holding it in the loose cradle of her other hand. It was puffy and bent at an odd angle from the joint. "He broke my fucking finger."

"It might be dislocated. I've done that before." Val remembered falling on her own hands on the lacrosse field, slipping out of a tree, trips to the doctor with his iodine and cigar-smoke smell. "You have to align it and splint it."

"Hey," Lolli said sharply. "I never asked for you to be my knight in shining armor. I can take care of myself. You didn't have to promise anything to that monster and you don't have to play doctor now."

"You're right." Val kicked a crushed aluminum can, watching it bounce across the street like a stone might skim over water. "You don't need any help. You have everything under control."

Lolli looked intently into the window of an electronics store where televisions showed their faces. "I didn't say that."

Val bit her lip, tasting the remains of the troll's solution. She remembered his golden eyes and the rich, hot rage in his voice. "I'm sorry. I should have just believed you."

"Yeah, you should have," Lolli said, but she smiled.

"Look, we can get a stick or something for the splint. Tie it off with a shoelace." Val squatted down and started unlacing her sneaker.

"I have a better idea," Lolli said, turning toward the mouth of an alley. "How about I forget about the pain?" She sat down against the filthy bricks and pulled out her soup spoon, needle, lighter, and a glassine bag of whatever-it-was from her pack. "Give me the shoelace anyway."

Val thought of the moving shadows, remembered the amber sand, and had no idea what might happen next. "What is that?"

"Nevermore," Lolli said. "That's what Luis calls it, because there're three rules: Never more than once a day, never more than a pinch at a time, and never more than two days in a row."

"Who made those up?"

"Dave and Luis, I think. After they were living on the street, Luis started couriering for more faeries—I guess they have errands they need someone to run—and Dave took over some of the deliveries. One time he took a little bit of the Never, stirred it into some water like they do, and drank it up. It gives the faeries more glamour or something, to keep the iron from affecting them so much, but it gets us high. Drinking it was okay for a while, but it's so much better when you shoot it in your arm or freebase it like Dave does." Lolli spat into the spoon and lit the lighter. The solution sparkled as though it had just come alive.

"Glamour?"

"The way they make themselves look different, or other things seem different. Magic, I guess."

"What's it like?"

"Never? Like the ocean breaking over your head and sweeping you out to sea," Lolli said. "Nothing else can touch you. Nothing else matters."

Lolli drew up the stuff with the needle. Val wondered if she could ever feel that nothing touched her. It sounded like oblivion. It sounded like peace.

"No," Val said, and Lolli stopped.

Val smiled. "Do me first."

"Really?" Lolli grinned. "You want to?"

Val nodded, unbending her arm and holding it out.

Lolli tied off Val's arm, tapped out the bubbles from the syringe, and slid the needle in as neatly as if Val's skin had been built to sheathe it. The pain was so slight, it was less than the nick of a razor.

"You know," Lolli said, "the thing about drugs is that they make things kind of shift, go leftward and sideways and upside down, but with Never, you can take everyone else upside down with you. What else can do that?"

Val had never thought too much about the inside of her elbow, but now it felt as vulnerable as her wrist, as her throat. She rubbed the bruise left when the needle was gone. There was barely any blood. "I don't know. Nothing, I guess."

Lolli nodded, as though pleased with that answer. As she was cooking up another batch of Never, Val found herself distracted by the sound of the fire, the feel of her own veins squirming like a nest of snakes under her skin.

"I—," Val started, but euphoria melted her bones. The world turned to honey, thick and slow

holly black

and sweet. She couldn't think of what she wanted to say, and for a moment she imagined losing her words forever. What if she could never think of what it was she wanted to say?

"Your veins are drinking down the magic," Lolli said, her voice coming from a great distance. "Now you can make anything happen."

Fire flooded Val, washing away the cold, banishing all the small agonies—the blister on her toe, the ache of her stomach, the too-tight muscles across her shoulders. Her fear melted away, replaced with *power*. Power that throbbed inside of her, giddy and eager, opening her up like a puzzle box to find all of her secret hurt and anger and confusion. Power that whispered to her in tongues of fury, with promises of triumph.

"See? It doesn't hurt anymore," Lolli said. She took hold of her finger and twisted. It made a snapping sound, like the crack of a knuckle, and popped back into place.

Everything looked too clear, too bright. Val found herself getting lost in the patterns of grime on the sidewalk, the promise of candy-colored neon signs, the scent of distant pipe smoke, of exhaust pipes, of frying oil. Everything was strange and beautiful and swollen with possibilities.

Lolli grinned like a jackal. "I want to show you something."

The fire was eating away at the inside of her arms, painful, but deliciously so, like being flooded with light. She felt volatile and unstoppable.

"Is this how it always is?" Val asked, even though some distant part of her mind told her that it was impossible for Lolli to know what Val was feeling.

"Yes," Lolli said. "Oh, yes."

Lolli led them down the street, approaching an Asian man with close-cropped graying hair walking in the opposite direction. At first he backed up when they got close, but then something seemed to relax him.

"I'd like some money," Lolli said.

He smiled and reached into the pocket of his coat, pulling out a wallet. He took out several twenties. "Is this enough?" he asked. His voice sounded strange, soft, and dazzled.

She leaned in to kiss his cheek. "Thank you."

Val felt the wind whip off the Hudson, but the scorching cold couldn't touch her now. The fiercest gust seemed like a caress. "How did you make him do that?" she asked, but it was all wonder and no apprehension.

"He wanted to," Lolli said. "They all want us to have whatever we want."

holly black

As they walked, each person they passed gave them what they asked for. A woman in a sequined skirt gave them her last cigarette, a young guy in a baseball cap handed over his coat without a word, a woman in a bronze trench pulled a pair of glittering gold hoops right from her ears.

Lolli reached into a trash can and lifted out banana peels, wet paper, slimy bread, and cups filled with sludgy water. "Watch this," she said.

In her hands, the detritus turned into cupcakes so white and fine that Val reached out her hand for one.

"No," Lolli said. "For them." She handed one to an old man as he passed and he gobbled it like an animal, reaching for another and another as though they were the best food in the world.

Val laughed, partially at his delight, partially at their power over him. She picked up a stone and turned it into a cracker. He ate that too, licking Val's hands for any last trace of it. His tongue tickled and that only made her laugh harder.

They walked a few more blocks; Val couldn't be sure how many. She kept noticing fascinating things she hadn't seen before: the sheen on a roach's wings as it scuttled over a grate, the smirk of a carved face over a lintel, the broken stems of flowers outside of a bodega.

"Here we are," Lolli said, pointing to a dark store. In the window, mannequins posed in pencil skirts printed with scenes from comic books, or lounged on modern, red settees, holding up polka-dotted martini glasses. "I want to go in."

Val walked up to the window and kicked the glass. It spiderwebbed but didn't cave. The alarm squawked twice and went silent.

"Try this," Lolli instructed, picking up a plastic straw. In her hand, it changed into a crowbar, heavy and cold.

Val smiled with delight and hit the window with all the built-up aggression of hating Tom and her mother and herself, all the anger at the troll in the tower, and the fury at the entire universe. She beat the glass in until it folded like bent metal.

"Nice." Lolli grinned and crawled through the window. As soon as Val was inside, the glass was back, uncracked, better than new.

Inside the store, lights came on and canned music started to play.

Each new glamour seemed to feed the power inside of Val instead of depleting it. With each enchantment, she felt giddier, wilder. Val wasn't even quite sure which one of them was doing what anymore.

Lolli kicked off her shoes in the middle of the

store and tried on a dress of green satin. Val could see her bare feet were red with blisters. "Is this cute?"

"Sure." Val picked out a new pair of underwear and some jeans, tossing her old clothes onto the outstretched arm of a mannequin. "Look at this crap, Lolli. These are a-hundred-and-eighty-dollar jeans and they don't look like anything. They're just jeans."

"They're free," said Lolli.

Val found clothes and then sat down in one of the cartoonish armchairs to watch Lolli try on more things. As she danced around with a beaded shawl on her head, Val noticed the display next to the chair.

"See this?" Val said, holding up an avocado-colored wineglass. "How ugly is this? I mean, who would pay for something this ugly?"

Lolli grinned and reached for a hat with pink feather fringe. "People buy what they're told to buy. They don't know it's ugly, or maybe they do and they think there's something wrong with thinking that."

"Then they need to be protected from themselves," Val said, and hurled the glass at the linoleum tile. It shattered, glass shards spinning out in every direction. "Anyone can see these things are ugly. Ugly, ugly, ugly."

Lolli started to laugh and she kept on laughing as Val broke every last one.

Walking back to Worth Street station with Lolli, Val felt disoriented, unsure of what had actually happened. As the Never ebbed from her, she felt more and more faded, as though the fire of the enchantment had eaten away some tangible part of her, had harrowed her.

She remembered a store and people that ate food out of her hands, and walking, but she couldn't quite be sure where she'd gotten what she was wearing. She remembered a blur of faces and gifts and smiles, as hazy as the memory of a monster in a tower before all that.

When she looked down at herself, she saw clothes she couldn't remember picking out—big black ass-kicking boots that were definitely warmer than her sneakers, a T-shirt printed with a heraldic lion, black cargo pants with tons of zippered pockets and a black coat that was much too big for her. It unnerved her to think that her own clothes were just gone, left behind somewhere. The boots pinched her feet as she walked, but she was glad of the coat. It seemed like they'd walked far into SoHo and, without the magic in her body, she felt colder than ever.

As they slipped through the service entrance

and down the stairs, Val saw several people in the tunnel. The changing flicker of the candles lit up one of their cheekbones, the curve of a jaw, the paper bag–covered bottle one was lifting to his mouth. The girl with the swollen belly was there, wrapped up in a blanket with another body.

"There you are," Sketchy Dave said. His voice sounded slurred and when the candlelight caught him, she could see that his mouth had the slack look of the very drunk. "Come sit with me, Lolli," he said. "Come sit over here."

"No," she said, picking her way over to Luis instead. "You can't tell me what to do."

"I'm not trying to tell you anything," he said, and now his voice was miserable. "Don't you know I love you, baby? I would do anything for you. Look." He held up his arm. "Lolli" was carved into the skin in sluggishly bleeding letters. "Look what I did."

Val winced. Lolli just laughed.

Luis lit a cigarette and, for a moment, as the match struck, his whole face was illuminated. He looked furious.

"Why don't you believe me?" Dave demanded.

"I believe you," Lolli said, voice gone shrill. "I don't *care*. You're boring. Maybe I would love you if you weren't *boring*!"

Luis jumped to his feet, pointing his cigarette

first at Lolli and then at Dave. "Just shut the fuck up, both of you." He turned and glared at Val, as though this all was somehow her fault.

"Who are they?" Val asked, gesturing toward the couple tangled in the blankets. "I thought nobody was supposed to be down here."

"Nobody *is* supposed to be down here," he said, sitting down next to his brother. "Not you, not me, not them."

Val rolled her eyes, but she didn't think he noticed in the candlelight. Scooting close to Lolli, she whispered, "Is he this much of a dick when I'm not around?"

"It's complicated," Lolli whispered back. "They used to squat here before, but Derek got sent upstate for some shit and Tanya moved to some abandoned building out in Queens."

Luis shifted closer to his brother and spoke quietly to him. Sketchy Dave got up, hands fisted. "You get everything," he shouted at Luis, tears on his cheeks, snot running from his nose.

"What do you want from me?" Luis demanded. "I never touched that girl. It's not my fault you're whipped."

"I'm not a thing," Lolli yelled at both of them, a terrible expression on her face. "You can't talk about me like I'm a thing."

holly black

"Fuck you," Dave shouted. "I'm boring? I'm a coward? Someday you're going to wish you didn't talk that way."

The girl in the blanket sat up, blinking rapidly. "Wha—"

"Come on," Luis said, taking Dave's arm. "Let's get out of here, Dave. You're just drunk. You need to walk it off."

Dave jerked away from his brother. "Fuck off."

Val stood up, the last lingering threads of Never making the chalky dark of the tunnels swim. Her legs felt rubbery and the soles of her feet burned from all the walking her body was just starting to realize it had done, but the last thing she wanted was to get caught up in claustrophobic bullshit. "Never mind. We're out of here."

Lolli followed her back up the stairs.

"Why do you like him so much?" Val asked.

"I don't like him." Lolli didn't bother to ask who Val meant. "His eye is jacked up. He's too skinny and he acts like an old man."

Val shrugged and threaded her thumb through the belt loop of her new pants, watching her boots step on the cracks in the sidewalk, letting her silence speak for her.

Lolli sighed. "He should be begging me for it."

"He should," Val agreed.

They walked down Bayard Street, past groceries selling bags of rice, piles of pale golden apples, bamboo shoots in bowls of water, and huge spiky fruit that hung down from the ceiling. They passed little shops selling sunglasses, paper lamps, clumps of bamboo bound with gold ribbons, and bright-green plastic dragons molded to resemble carved jade.

"Let's stop," Lolli said. "I'm hungry."

The mere mention of food made Val's stomach growl. The fear had soured her belly and she realized she hadn't eaten anything since the night before. "Okay."

"I'll show you how to table-score."

Lolli picked a place where several ducks hung, necks bent around a wire, dripping with red glaze, empty pits where their eyes once were. Inside, people lined up to pick out food from an assortment of steaming dishes. Lolli ordered hot teas and egg rolls for both of them. The man behind the counter didn't seem to speak any English, but he dumped the right items onto their tray along with nearly a dozen plastic packets.

They slid into a booth. Lollie looked around, then ripped open a packet of duck sauce and squirted it on her roll, topping that with hot mustard. She

holly black

nodded her head casually in the direction of an empty booth with a few plates still on it. "See those leftovers?"

"Yeah," Val bit into her egg roll, grease slicking her lip. It was delicious.

"Hold on." Lolli got up, walked over to a half-eaten plate of lo mein, picked it up, and walked back to their table. "Table-score. See?"

Val snorted, slightly scandalized. "I can't believe you just did that."

Lolli smiled, but her smile faded into a weird expression. "Sometimes you wind up doing a lot of crazy stuff that you can't believe you did."

"I guess so," Val said slowly. After all, she couldn't believe that she'd spent the night in an abandoned subway station with a bunch of homeless kids. She couldn't believe that instead of screaming and crying when she'd found out about Tom and her mom, she'd shaved her head and gone to a hockey game. She couldn't believe that she was sitting there calmly eating someone else's dinner when she'd just seen a monster.

"I moved in with my boyfriend when I was thirteen," Lolli said.

"Really?" Val asked. The food going into her mouth was calming her, letting her believe that the world would go on, even if there were faeries and weird faerie drugs. There would still be Chinese food and it would still be hot and greasy and good.

Lolli made a face. "My boyfriend's name was Alex. He was twenty-two. My mom thought he was a pervert and told me not to see him. Eventually, I got sick of sneaking around and just took off."

"Shit," Val said, because she couldn't think of what else to say. When she was thirteen, boys had been as mysterious and unattainable as the stars in the sky. "What happened?"

Lolli took a couple of quick bites of lo mein and washed them down with tea. "Alex and I argued all the time. He was dealing out of the apartment and he didn't want me doing anything, even when he was shooting up right in front of me. He was worse than my parents. Finally, he found some other girl and just told me to get out."

"Did you go back home?" Val asked.

Lolli shook her head. "You can't go back," she said. "You change and you can't go back."

"I can go back," Val said automatically, but the memory of the troll and her bargain haunted her. It seemed unreal now, in the light and heat of the restaurant, but it nagged at the back of her thoughts.

holly black

Lolli paused for a moment, as if she were considering that. "You know what I did to Alex?" she asked, wicked smile returning. "I still had the keys. I went back when no one was there and I trashed the place. I threw everything out the window—his clothes, her clothes, the television, his drugs, every fucking thing I could get my hands on got dusted onto the street."

Val cackled with delight. She could just imagine Tom's face if she'd done that to him. She pictured his new computer cracked open on the driveway, iPod smashed into white pieces, black clothes spread out over the lawn.

"Soooo," Lolli said with a mock innocent look. "You enjoyed that story way too much not to have an asshole-boyfriend story of your own."

Val opened her mouth, not sure what she was going to say. The words stalled on her tongue. "My boyfriend was sleeping with my mom," she finally forced out.

Lolli laughed until she was choking, then stared at Val for a moment, eyes wide and incredulous. "Really?" she asked.

"Really," Val said, strangely satisfied that she'd managed to shock even Lolli. "They thought I got on the train and they were making out on the couch. Her lipstick was all over his face."

"Oh, nasty! *Nasty!*" Lolli's mouth contorted with honest, giggling disgust. Val laughed too, because, suddenly, it *was* funny. Val laughed so hard that her stomach hurt, that she couldn't breathe, that tears leaked out to wet her cheeks. It was exhausting to laugh like that, but she felt like she was waking from a strange dream.

"Are you really going back home to *that*?" Lolli asked.

Val was still half-drunk with laughter. "I have to, don't I? I mean, even if I stayed here for a while, I can't live the rest of my life in a tunnel." Realizing what she'd said, she glanced up at Lolli, expecting her to be insulted, but she just leaned her head on her hands and looked thoughtful.

"You should call your mom, then," Lolli said finally. She pointed toward the lobby. "There's a pay phone out there."

Val was shocked. It was the last piece of advice she expected to get from Lolli. "I've got my cell."

"So call your mom already."

Val fished out her cell phone with a feeling of dread and turned it on. The screen flashed, calls missed count climbing. It stopped at sixty-seven. She'd only gotten one text. It was from Ruth and read: "where r u? your moms going crazy."

Val hit reply. "Am still in city," she typed, but

then she stopped, not sure what to write next. What was she going to do next? Could she really go home?

Bracing, she clicked over to voice mail. The first message was from her mom, her voice soft and strangled sounding: "Valerie, where are you? I just want to know you're safe. It's very late and I called Ruth. She told me what she said. I-I-I don't know how to explain what happened or to say how sorry I am." There was a long pause. "I know you're very mad at me. You have every right to be mad at me. Just please let someone know you're all right."

It was weird to hear her mother's voice after all this time. It made her gut clench with hurt and fury and acute embarrassment. Sharing a boy with her mom stripped her deeper than bare. She deleted it and clicked to the next message. It was from Val's dad: "Valerie? Your mother is very concerned. She said that you two had a fight and you ran off. I know how your mother can be, but staying out all night isn't helping anything. I thought you were smarter than this." In the background, she could hear her half sisters shrieking over the sound of cartoons.

An unfamiliar man's voice spoke next. He sounded bored. "Valerie Russell? This is Officer

Montgomery. Your mother reported you as missing after a disagreement the two of you had. Nobody is going to make you do anything you don't want to do, but I really need you to give me a call and let me know that you're not in any trouble." He left a number.

The next message was a silence punctuated by several wet-sounding sobs. After a few moments, her mother's choked voice wailed, "Where are you?"

Val clicked off. It was horrible to listen to how upset her mother was. She should go home. Maybe it would be okay—if she never brought a boyfriend to the house, if her mom would just stay out of her way for a while. It would be less than a year before Val was out of high school. Then she wouldn't ever have to live there again.

She scrolled to "home" and pressed the call button. The phone on the other end rang as Val's fingers turned to ice. Lolli arranged the remaining lo mein noodles into the shape of something that might have been the sun, a flower, or a really poorly rendered lion.

"Hello," Val's mother said, her voice low. "Honey?"

Val hung up. The cell rang almost immediately and she turned it off.

holly black

"You knew I couldn't do it," she accused Lolli. "Didn't you?"

Lolli shrugged. "Better to find out now. It's a long way to go just to come back."

Val nodded, afraid in a new, acute way. For the first time she realized that she might never be ready to go home.

Chapter 6

*Reality is that which, when you stop believing in it,
doesn't go away.*

—PHILIP K. DICK

Val woke to the shriek of a train barreling past. Sweat stuck the wool coat to her clammy skin, despite the cold. Her head throbbed, her mouth burned, and even with all the food she'd eaten the night before, she felt ravenous. Shivering, she wrapped the covering tighter around herself and curled her legs closer to her body.

She tried to think back, past the table-scored food and the phone call home. There had been a monster and a sword made of glass, then a needle in her arm and a rush of power that still filled her with longing. She scrambled into a sitting position, looking down at new clothes that proved her memories were not formed only from bits of half-remembered dreams. Dave's arm had bled and strangers had done whatever she told them and magic was real. She reached for her backpack, relieved that she hadn't left that somewhere along with the rest of her clothes.

Only Lolli was still sleeping, curled up in the fetal position, a new dress layered over a skirt and a new pair of jeans. Dave and Luis weren't there.

"Lolli?" Val crawled over and shook Lolli's shoulder.

Lolli turned, pushed blue hair out of her face, and made a small, irritated noise. Her breath was sour. "Go away," she slurred, pulling the stained blanket over her face.

Val stood up unsteadily. Her vision swam. She picked up her backpack and forced herself to walk through the darkness up onto the night streets of Manhattan. The evening skies were bright with clouds and the air was thick with ozone, as if there was a storm blowing in fast.

She felt dried up and cracked and fragile as one of the few leaves that blew out from the park. It seemed that if you stripped away all the sports and the school and the normal life, what was within her wasn't much at all. Her body felt bruised, as though something else had been riding around in her skin the night before, something so awful and vast that it had charred her insides. There was a feeling of satisfaction, though, in spite of the fear. *I did this,* she thought, *I did this to myself.*

Deep breaths of cold air settled her stomach, but her mouth just got hotter.

The creature's words came back to her unbidden: "You serve me for a month. Each dusk you will go to Seward Park. There, you will find a note under the wolf's paw. If you do not do what it says, things will go hard with you." She was already late.

Val thought of the slick solution the troll had spread over her skin and felt a tremor shoot through her, an electric charge that jolted her hand to her lips. They were dry and swollen to the touch, but she found no cut or wound to explain the stinging.

She walked into a deli and bought a cup of ice water with some of the change at the bottom of her bag, hoping that it might cool her mouth. Outside the shop, she sat down on the concrete and sucked a cube of ice into her mouth, her hand shaking so much that she was afraid to take a sip.

A woman coming out of the liquor store next door glanced down at Val and dropped some change into Val's cup of water. Val looked up, startled and ready to protest, but the woman had already walked on.

By the time Val removed the folded paper from under the wolf's paw, her whole mouth was sore as a wound. She squatted near the dried-up fountain and leaned her head against a chipped bar of metal fencing as her fingers numbly opened the paper.

She half-expected a blank page she'd have to crumple and toss, like the one Dave had gotten, but there were words, written in the same looping hand that had addressed the bottle of amber sand:

"Come beneath the support of the Manhattan Bridge and knock thrice on the tree that squats where no tree should."

She jammed the note into her pocket, but as she did, her hand bumped something else. She pulled it out—a silver money clip with a huge, rough piece of turquoise at its center, the clasp stuffed with a twenty, two fives, and at least a dozen singles.

Had she taken the money? Had Lolli? Val couldn't remember. She'd never stolen anything before. One time she'd walked out of a Spencers in the mall with a Rangers poster in her hand, not realizing she hadn't paid for it until she and her friends reached the escalators. Her friends were impressed so she acted as if she'd done it on purpose, but afterward she felt so bad that she never hung it.

Val tried to think back to the night before, to the terrible things she must have done, but it was as if she were remembering a story told by someone else. It was all a blur that, despite everything, made her skin itch for Nevermore.

She started walking, in too much pain to do anything else. Dread coiled in her stomach. She started down Market, passing Asian stores and a bubble tea place with a group of teenagers standing in front of it, all talking over one another and laughing. Val felt as disconnected from them as if she were a hundred years old. She reached for her backpack, wanting more than anything to call Ruth, wanting to hear someone who knew her, someone who could remind her of that old self. But her mouth hurt too much.

Cutting across onto Cherry, she walked a little farther, close enough to the East River that no buildings blocked her view. The water shone with the reflected radiance of the bridge and the far shore. A barge nearly became a mass of negative space except for a few lights glittering at the prow.

The bridge loomed directly ahead of her, the

supports each like the tower of a castle, rough stonework rising high above the street, ruddy with runoff from rust on the metal supports above. The stretch of rock was interrupted by casement windows high above the street.

Broken glass crunched beneath Val's boots as she passed under the graceful arch of the underpass. The sidewalk stank of stale urine and something rotting. On one side was a makeshift wire fence, blocking the way into a construction area where a mound of sand waited to be spread. On the other, close to where she walked, was what looked like a bricked-up doorway. Below it, Val saw the stump of a tree, its roots digging deep into the concrete.

"The tree." Val kicked the stump softly. The wood was wet and dark with filth, but the roots sank down into the concrete sidewalk, as though they stretched past the tunnels and pipes, worming their way into some secret, rich soil. She wondered if this was the same tree that bloomed with pale fruit.

It was an eerie thing to see a stump here, nestled up against a building as if they were kin. But perhaps no eerier than the idea that she'd fallen into a fairy tale. In a video game, there would have been some pixelated storm of color and maybe even an on-screen message warning her that she was leaving the real world behind. *Portal to Faerieland. Do you want to go through? Y/N.*

Val knelt down and rapped three times on the stump. The wet wood barely made a sound under her knuckles. A spider scuttled out toward the street.

A sharp noise made Val look up. A fracture appeared in the stone above the stump, as though something had struck it. She stood and reached out to run her finger across the line, but as she touched the wall, patches of stone cracked and fell away, until there was a rough doorframe.

She stepped through onto the stairwell, steps extending up and down from the landing. When she looked back, the wall was solid. A sudden burst of terror nearly overwhelmed her and only pain held her in place.

Trip trap.

"Hello?" she called up the steps. It hurt to move her mouth.

Trip trap.

The troll appeared on the landing.

Who's trip trapping over my bridge?

"Most people would have come sooner." His rough, gravelly voice filled the stairway. "How your mouth must hurt to bring you here at last."

holly black

"It wasn't so bad," she said, trying not to wince.

"Come up, little liar." Ravus turned and walked back to his rooms. She hurried up the dusty stairs.

The large loftlike space flickered with fat candles set on the floor, their glow making her shadow jump on the walls, huge and terrible. Trains rumbled above them and cold air rushed in through covered windows.

"Here." In the palm of one six-fingered hand, he held a small, white stone. "Suck on it."

She snatched the stone and popped it in her mouth, in enough pain not to question him. It felt cool on her tongue and tasted like salt at first and then like nothing at all. The pain abated slowly and with it, the last of the nausea, but she found exhaustion taking its place. "What do you want me to do?" she asked, pushing the rock into her cheek with her tongue so she could talk.

"For now, you can shelve a few books." Turning, he went to his desk and began to strain the liquid from a small copper pot thick with sticks and leaves. "There may be an order to them, but since I have lost the understanding of it, I don't expect you to find one. Put them where they will fit."

Val lifted one of the volumes off a dusty pile.

The book was heavy, the leather on it cracked and worn along the binding. She flipped it open. The pages were hand lettered and there were watercolor and ink drawings of plants on most of the pages. "Amaranth," she read silently. "Weave it into a crown to speed the healing of the wearer. If worn as a wreath, confers invisibility instead." She closed the book and pushed it into the plywood and brick shelves.

Val rolled the stone around in her mouth like a candy as she put away the troll's scattered tomes. She took in the mishmash of moth-eaten army blankets, stained carpet, and ripped garbage bags that served as curtains not even the outside streetlights could pierce. A dainty flowered teacup, half full of a brackish liquid, rested beside a ripped leather chair. The idea of the troll holding the delicate cup in his claws made her snort with laughter.

"To know your target's weakness, that is the intuitive genius of great liars," said the troll without looking up. His voice was dry. "Though the Folk differ greatly, one from another and from place to place, we are alike in this: We cannot outright speak what is untrue. I find myself fascinated by lies, however, even to the point of wanting to believe them."

She didn't reply.

"Do you consider yourself skilled in lying?" he asked.

"Not really," Val said. "I'm more of an accomplished sucker."

He said nothing to that.

Picking up another book, Val noticed the glass sword hanging on the wall. The blade was newly cleaned and looking through it, she could see the stone, each pit in the rock magnified and distorted as though it was under water.

"Is it made from spun sugar?" His voice was close by and she realized how long she'd been staring at the sword. "Ice? Crystal? Glass? That's what you're wondering, isn't it? How something that looks so fragile is so hard to break?"

"I was just thinking how beautiful it was," Val said.

"It's a cursed thing."

"Cursed?" Val echoed.

"It failed a dear friend of mine and cost him his life." He ran one hooked nail down the length of it. "A better blade might have stopped his opponent."

"Who . . . who was his opponent?" she asked.

"I was," the troll said.

"Oh." Val could think of no reply. Although he seemed calm now, even kind, she heard the warning in his words. She thought of something her mother had told her when she'd finally broken up with one of her most dysfunctional boyfriends. *When a man tells you he's going to hurt you, believe it. They always warn you and they're always right.* Val pushed the words out of her head; she didn't want any of her mother's advice.

The troll walked back to the table and picked up three waxed and stoppered beer bottles. Through the amber glass she couldn't see the color of the contents, but the idea that it might be that very same amber sand that ran through her veins the night before made her skin thrill with possibility.

"The first delivery will be in Washington Square Park, to a trio of fey there." One hooked nail pointed to a map of the five boroughs and most of New York and New Jersey taped on the wall. She walked closer to it, noticing for the first time that there were thin black pins stuck into various points along the surface. "The second can be left outside of an abandoned building, here. That . . . recipient may not wish to show himself. I want you to take the third to an abandoned park, here." The troll seemed to be indicating a street in Williamsburg. "There are small grassy hills, close to the rocks and the water. The creature that you seek will wait for you at the river's edge."

holly black

"What are the pins for?" Val asked.

He gave the map a quick sideways look and seemed to hesitate before speaking again. "Deaths. It isn't unusual for the Folk to die in cities—most of us here are in exile or in hiding from other fey. Living so close to so much iron is dangerous. One would only do it for the protection it affords. But these deaths are different. I'm trying to puzzle them out."

"What am I delivering?"

"Medicine," he said. "Useless to you, but it eases the pain of the Folk exposed to so much iron."

"Am I suppose to collect anything from them?"

"Don't concern yourself with that," said the troll.

"Look," Val said. "I'm not trying to be difficult, but I never lived in New York before. I mean, I've been up here for things and I've walked around the Village, but I can't find all these places with a glance at a map."

He laughed. "Of course not. Had you hair, I would give you three knots, one for each delivery, but since you don't, give me your hand."

She held it out, palm up, ready to snatch it back if he took out anything sharp.

Reaching into one of the pockets of his coat,

the troll drew out a spool of green thread. "Your left hand," he said.

She gave him her other hand and watched as he wound her first, middle, and ring fingers with the string, tying one knot on each digit. "What is this supposed to do?" she asked.

"It will help you make your deliveries."

She nodded, looking at her fingers. How could this be magic? She'd expected something that glittered and glowed, not mundane stuff. String was just string. She wanted to ask about it again, but she thought it might be rude, so she asked something else she'd been wondering about. "Why does iron bother faeries?"

"We don't have it in our blood like you do. More than that, I don't know. There was a king of the Unseelie Court poisoned with but a few shards quite recently. His name was Nephamael and he thought to make an ally of iron—he wore a band of it at his brow, letting the burns scar deep until his flesh was so toughened it could scar no more. But that did not toughen his throat. He died choking on the stuff."

"What are these Courts?" Val asked.

"When there are enough faeries in an area they often organize themselves into groups. You might call them gangs, but the Folk usually call

holly black

them Courts. They occupy some territory, often fighting with other nearby Courts. There are Seelie Courts, which we call Bright Courts, and the Unseelie Courts, or Night Courts. You might, at first glance, think that the Bright Courts were good and the Night Courts evil, but you would be much, although not entirely, mistaken."

Val shuddered. "Am I going to be doing deliveries alone? Are any of the others coming with me?"

His golden eyes glittered in the firelight. "Others? Luis is the only human courier I've ever had. Is there someone else you are thinking of?"

Val shook her head, not sure what she should say.

"It doesn't matter. I would ask that you do these tasks alone and that you do not speak of them with any of the . . . *others*."

"Okay," Val said.

"You are under my protection," he said, letting her take the bottle. "Still, there are things I would have you know about the fey. Do not tarry with them and take nothing they offer, especially food." She thought of the magiced stone she had fed to an old man and nodded grimly, guiltily. "Put this comfrey in your shoe. It will help you keep safe and speed your travel. And here's madwort to keep you from fascination. You can tuck that into your pocket."

Val took the plants, toed off her left boot, and tucked the comfrey inside. She could feel it there, nestled against her sock, oddly comforting and alarming because it was comforting.

When she emerged on the street again, she felt a tug from the thread twined around her first finger. Magic! It made her smile despite everything else as she started in that direction.

It was still early evening when she made it to Washington Square Park. She'd stopped along the way and spent stolen money on a ham sandwich that she was still too sick to digest, despite her hunger, and had to toss it away half-eaten. She'd even managed to wash her face in an icy fountain, where the water tasted of rust and pennies.

The three bottles of whatever-they-were clanked together in her backpack, heavier than they would have been if she hadn't been so tired. She longed to uncork one and taste the contents, to bring back the power and fearlessness of the night before, but she was wary enough of her exhaustion today that she didn't.

Walking through the park, past NYU students in bright scarves, past people hurrying to dinner or walking their tiny, sweatered dogs, she realized that she had no idea what she was looking

holly black

for. The thread pulled her toward a pack of middle-schoolers in expensive skater clothes climbing up on one of the interior fences. One floppy-haired boy in low-slung jeans, skull-print knee pads and checkerboard Vans was louder than the rest, standing on the top rung and whooping at three girls leaning against the thick trunk of a tree. They all had bare feet and hair the color of honey.

The thread all but dragged her to the three girls before it unraveled.

"Um, hi," Val said. "I have something of yours, I think."

"I can smell the glamour on you, thick and sweet," said one. Her eyes were gray as lead. "If you're not careful, a girl like you could get carried off under the hill. We'd leave a bit of wood behind and everyone would weep over it, because they'd be too stupid to know the difference."

"Don't be awful to her," said another, twirling a lock of hair around her hand. "She can't help being blind and dumb."

"Here," Val said, pushing the bottle into the hands of the one that hadn't spoken. "Take your medicine like good little girls."

"Ooooh, it has a tongue," said the girl with the gray eyes.

The third girl just smiled and glanced at the boy on the fence.

One of the others followed her look. "He's a pretty one," she said.

Val could barely tell the girls apart. They all had long, willowy limbs and hair that seemed to move with the slightest breeze. With their thin clothes and unshod feet, they should have been cold, but she could see they weren't.

"Do you want to dance with us?" a faerie girl asked Val.

"*He* wants to dance with us." The gray-eyed faerie gave the loud skater boy a wide grin.

"Come dance with us, messenger," said the third, speaking for the first time. Her voice was like a frog croaking and when she spoke, Val saw that her tongue was black.

"No," Val said, thinking of the troll's warnings and the madwort in her pocket. "I have to go."

"That's all right," said the gray-eyed faerie, toeing the earth with one bare foot. "You'll visit us again when you aren't so gaudy with spells. At least I hope you will. You're almost as pretty as he is."

"I'm not pretty at all," said Val.

"Suit yourself," said the girl.

• • •

She wasn't sure what she should expect to find as she passed by boarded-up tenement houses and bodegas with broken front windows. The building that the string on her finger tugged her toward was boarded up, too, and Val was surprised to see a garden blooming on the roof. Long tendrils of plants hung over the side and what looked like half-grown trees sprouted from what must have been thin soil, all of it trapped by an aluminum cage that capped the building. Val walked up to the entrance, now overgrown with ivy. On the second floor, the windows were completely missing, gaping holes in the brick, and she could almost see the rooms inside.

As she stepped onto the cracked front steps, the thread untied itself from her middle finger to drop into the nearby grass.

She took out the bottle from her backpack and set it down, thinking of the troll's directions.

Something rustled in the grass and Val yelped, jumping back, suddenly aware of how strangely quiet things had gotten. The cars still streaked by and the city sounds were still there, but they had faded somehow. A brown rat poked its head out of the grass, beady black eyes like polished pebbles, pink nose twitching. Val laughed with relief.

"Hey there," she said, squatting down. "I hear that you can bite through copper. That's really something."

The rat turned and scurried back through the grass as Val watched. A figure moved out of the shadows to scoop up the rodent and set it on a wide shoulder.

"Who . . . ," Val said and stopped herself.

He stepped into the light, a creature nearly as tall as the troll and thicker, with horns that curved back from his head like a ram's and a thick brown beard that ran to green at the tips. He was clad in a patchwork coat and hand-stitched boots.

"Come inside and warm up," he said, picking up the corked beer bottle. "I have some questions for you."

Val nodded, but her gaze slid toward the street, wondering if she could run for it. The faerie's hand came down hard on her shoulder, deciding the question. He steered her around the back of the building and through a door that hung by only the top hinge.

Inside the building were an array of mannequin parts, stacked unnervingly along the walls, a pyramid of heads in one corner and a wall of arms in multiple skin tones in another. A pile of wigs sat like a large, resting animal in the middle of the floor.

holly black

A tiny creature with moth wings buzzed through the air, holding a needle, and settling on a man's torso to sew a vest to the body.

Val looked around, afraid, noting anything that could be a weapon, backing up so her fingers could reach behind her and grab. She didn't like the idea of swinging a plastic leg at the creature, but if she had to, she would, even if she had no hope of it doing much damage. But as her fingers closed on what she thought was a whole arm, the mannequin hand came off in hers. "What is all this?" she asked loudly, hoping the faerie wouldn't notice.

"I make stock," said the horned creature, sitting down on a milk crate that bowed with his weight. "Me and Needlenix, we're the best you're like to find this side of the sea."

The moth-winged faerie buzzed. Val tried to put the hand back on the shelf behind her, but without looking, she couldn't seem to find a place for it. She settled for tucking it into her back pocket, under her coat.

"The Queen of the Seelie Court, Silarial herself, uses our work."

"Wow," Val said, as he clearly wanted her to be impressed. Then, in the silence that followed, she was obliged to ask, "Stock?"

He smiled and she could see that his teeth were yellowed and quite pointed. "It's what we leave behind when we steal someone away. Now, your logs or sticks or whatever, they work all right, but these mannequins are superior in every way. More convincing, even to those rare humans with a little bit of magic or Sight. Of course, I suppose that's cold comfort to you."

"I suppose it is," Val said. She thought of the girls in the park saying *We'd leave a bit of wood behind*. Was that what they'd meant?

"Of course, sometimes we leave one of our own to pretend to be the human child, but that silliness doesn't concern me." He looked at her. "We can be cruel to those that cross us. We blight crops, dry up the milk in a mother's breast, and wither limbs for the merest of slights. But sometimes I've thought that we are worse to those who have won our favor.

"Now, tell me," he said, sitting up and reaching for the potion bottle. In the firelight, she saw that his eyes were completely black, like his rat's. "Is this poison?"

"I don't know what it is," Val said. "I didn't make it."

"There have been quite a few deaths among the Folk."

"I heard something about that."

He grunted. "All of them were using Ravus's solution to stave off the iron sickness. All of them had deliveries from a courier just like yourself near their time of death."

Val thought of the incense man of a few days before. What was it he'd said? *Tell your friends to be careful whom they serve.* "You think Ravus . . ." She let the name sit in her mouth for a moment. "You think Ravus is the poisoner?"

"I don't know what I think," the horned man said. "Well, be on your way, then, courier. I'll find you again if I need to."

Val left quickly.

Passing an old theater, Val was drawn by the smell of popcorn and promise of heat. She could feel the roll of money in the pocket of her coat, more than enough to go inside, and yet the idea of seeing a movie seemed unimaginable, as though she would have to cross some impossible dimensional barrier between this life and the old one to sit in front of a screen.

When she was younger, Val and her mother had gone to movies every Sunday. First they would go to the one that Val wanted to see and then the one her mother chose. It usually wound up being something like a zombie film followed by a tearjerker. They would sit in the darkened theater and whisper to each other: *I bet he's the one that did it. She's going to die next. How can anyone be so stupid?*

She walked closer to the posters, just to be contrary. Most of what was playing were art films she hadn't heard of, but one called "Played" caught her eye. The poster showed an attractive guy posing as the jack of hearts, a tattoo of a red heart drawn on his bare shoulder. He was holding a page of cups card.

Val thought of Tom, dealing out his tarot deck into patterns on her kitchen counter. "This is what crosses you," he'd said, turning over a card with the image of a blindfolded woman holding swords in both her hands. "Two of swords."

"No one can tell the future," Val had said. "Not with something you can buy at Barnes and Noble."

Her mother had walked over to them and smiled down at Tom. "Will you do my cards?" she'd asked.

Tom had grinned back and they'd started talking about ghosts and crystals and psychic shit. Val should have known right then. But she'd poured a glass of soda, perched on a stool, and watched as Tom read a future for her mother in which he would have a part.

holly black

She walked up the steps, bought a ticket for the midnight show and walked into the café area. It was deserted. An array of small, metal tables with marble tops surrounded a pair of brown leather couches. Val flopped down on one sofa and stared up at the single chandelier glittering in the center of the room, hanging from a mural of the sky. She rested there, watching it glitter for a few moments and enjoying the luxury of heat before she forced herself into the bathroom. There was a half hour before the movie started and she wanted to get cleaned up.

Wadding up paper towels, Val gave herself a half-decent sponge bath, scrubbing her underpants with soap before putting them back on damp, and gargling mouthfuls of water. Then, sitting down in one of the stalls, she leaned her head against the painted metal wall and closed her eyes, letting the hot air from the ducts wash over her. *Just a moment,* she told herself. *I'll get up in just a moment.*

A woman with dark eyes and a thin face leaned over her. "*Pardon?*"

Val leaped to her feet and the cleaning woman backed away from her with a yelp, mop held out in front of her.

Embarrassed and stumbling, Val grabbed her backpack and rushed for the exit. She pushed through the metal doors as the suit-clad ushers started toward her.

Disoriented, Val saw that it was still dark. Had she missed the movie? Had she been asleep for only a moment?

"What time is it?" she demanded from a couple trying to flag down a cab.

The woman looked at her watch nervously, as though Val was going to snatch it off her wrist. "Almost three."

"Thanks," Val muttered. Although she'd gotten less than four hours of sleep sitting on a toilet, now that she was walking again, she found that she felt far better. The dizziness was almost gone and the smell of Asian food from an all-night restaurant a few blocks away made her stomach rumble in hunger.

She started walking in the direction of the smell.

A black SUV with tinted windows pulled up next to her, windows down. Two guys were sitting in the front seats.

"Hey," the guy on the passenger side said. "You know where the Bulgarian disco is? I thought it was off Canal, but now we're all turned around."

holly black

He had blond streaks in his carefully gelled hair.

Val shook her head. "It's probably closed by now anyway."

The driver leaned over. He was dark-haired and dark-skinned, with large, liquid eyes. "We're just looking to party. You like to party?"

"No," Val said. "I'm just going to get some food." She pointed toward the mock-Japanese exterior of the restaurant, glad it wasn't that far off, but painfully aware of the deserted streets between her and it.

"I could go for some fried rice," said the blond. The SUV rolled forward, keeping up with her as she walked. "Come on, we're just regular guys. We're not freaks or anything."

"Look," Val said. "I don't want to party, okay? Just let me alone."

"Okay, okay." The blond looked at his friend, who shrugged. "Can we at least give you a ride? It's not safe for you to be out here walking around on your own."

"Thanks, but I'm okay." Val wondered if she could outrun them, wondered if she should just take off and get a head start. But she kept walking, as if she weren't scared, as if they were only two nice, concerned guys trying to talk her into their truck.

She had comfrey in her shoe and madwort in her pocket and a plastic hand under the back of her shirt, but she wasn't sure how any of those things could help her.

The doors clicked unlocked as the truck rolled to a stop and she made a decision. Turning toward the open window, she smiled and said, "What makes you think I'm not one of the dangerous people?"

"I'm sure you're dangerous," said the driver, all smiles and insinuation.

"What if I told you that I just cut off some chick's hand?" Val said.

"What?" The blond guy looked at her in confusion.

"No, really. See?" Val pitched the mannequin hand through the window. It landed in the driver's lap.

The truck swerved and the blond yelped.

Val took off across the street, sprinting toward the restaurant.

"Fucking freak," the blond shouted as they pulled away from the curb, tires squealing.

Val's heart was beating double time as she walked into the safe heat of Dojo. Sitting down at a table with a sigh of relief, she ordered a huge bowl of steaming miso soup, cold sesame noodles dripping with peanut glaze, and ginger fried chicken that she ate with her fingers. When she was done, she thought she would fall asleep again, right at the table.

But she had one more delivery to do.

The street looked mostly unused and the sides of it were strewn with trash—broken glass, dried condoms, a ripped pair of pantyhose. Still, the smell of dew on the pavement, on the rust of the fence and the sparse grass, along with the empty streets made Williamsburg seem far away from Manhattan.

She ducked under a chain-link fence. The lot was empty, but she could see a ditch between the cracked concrete and the small hills. She stepped into it, using it like a path to walk out to where black rocks marked the space between the beach and the river.

Something was there. At first Val thought it was a lump of drying seaweed, a stray plastic bag, but as she got closer she realized it was a woman with green hair, lying facedown on the rocks, half in and half out of the water. Rushing over, Val saw the flies buzzing around the woman's torso and her tail drifting with the current, scales catching the streetlights to shine like silver.

It was the corpse of a mermaid.

Chapter 7

To these I turn, in these I trust—
Brother Lead and Sister Steel.

—SIEGFRIED SASSOON,
THE OLD HUNTSMAN AND OTHER POEMS

The first time Val saw anything dead was at the mall by her dad's house when she was twelve. She'd tossed a penny into the fountain by the food court and wished for a pair of running shoes. A few minutes later, she reconsidered and rushed back to try and find her coin and do the wish over. But what she saw, floating on the still water, was the limp body of a sparrow. She'd reached in and lifted it up and water had poured out of its tiny beak like from a cup. It smelled awful, like meat left in the refrigerator to defrost and forgotten. She had stared at it a moment before she realized it was dead.

As Val ran through the streets and over the

Manhattan Bridge, breath gusting into the air, she thought of the little drowned bird. Now she'd seen two dead things.

The magical doorway under the bridge opened the same way that it had last time, but as she stepped onto the dark landing, she saw she wasn't alone. Someone was heading down the steps, and it was only when the candle he cradled made the silver loops through his lip and nose glitter and the white of his eyes shine that she realized it was Luis. He looked as startled as she was and in that uncertain light, exhausted.

"Luis?" Val asked.

"I hoped that you were long gone." Luis's voice was soft and remorseless. "I hoped that you ran back to Mommy and Daddy in the suburbs. That's all you bridge-and-tunnel girls know—running away when things get tough. Run to the big bad city and then run home."

"Fuck you," Val said. "You know nothing about me."

"Well, you don't know shit about me, either. You think I've been a dick to you, but I've done you nothing but favors."

"What is your problem with me? You hated me the minute I showed up!"

"Any friend of Lolli's is going to stir shit up,

and that's just what you did. And here I am, getting interrogated by an angry troll because of you two bitches. What do you think my problem is?"

Anger made Val's face hot, even in the cold stairwell. "I think this: The only thing special about you is that you have the Sight. You talk shit about faeries, but you love that you're the one who can see them. That's why you're disgustingly jealous of anyone else that so much as talks to one."

Luis gaped at her as if he'd been slapped.

Words fell from Val's mouth before she even realized what she was about to say. "And I think something else, too. Rats might be able to chew their way through copper or whatever, but the only reason they survive is because there are bazillions of them. That's what's so special about rats— they fuck all the time and have a million rat babies."

"Stop," Luis said, holding up his hand as if to ward off her words. His voice dropped low, the anger seeming to go out of him like a popped balloon. "Fine. Yeah. To Ravus and the rest of the faerie folk, that's all humans are—pathetic things that breed like crazy and die so fast you can't tell the difference between one and another. Look, I have spent the past I don't know how long answering questions after drinking some

holly black

kind of noxious crap that made me tell the truth. All because of you and Lolli breaking in here. I'm tired and I'm pissed." He rubbed his face with his hand. "You're not the first straggler that Lolli brought home, you know. You don't understand what you're playing around with."

Val was unnerved by the sudden change in Luis's tone. "What do you mean?"

"There was another girl a couple of months ago—another stray Lolli decided to bring underground. It was when Lolli first got the idea that they could inject the potions. Lolli and the girl, Nancy, wanted to cop some dope, but didn't have any money. Then Lolli started talking about what else they could shoot and they did some of the stuff from one of Dave's deliveries. All of a sudden, they start talking like they can see things that aren't there and, even worse, Dave starts seeing the shit, too. Nancy got hit by a train and she was grinning right up until it hit her."

Val looked away from the flickering candle, into the darkness. "That sounds like an accident."

"Of course it was a fucking accident. But Lolli loved the stuff, even after that. She got Dave to do it."

"Did she know what it was?" Val asked. "Did she know about the faeries? About Ravus?"

"She knew. I told Dave about Ravus because Dave's my brother, even though he's an idiot. He told Lolli because she's a tease and he would do anything to impress her. And Lolli told Nancy, because Lolli can't keep her fucking mouth shut."

Val could hear Lolli's brittle laugh in her mind. "What's the big deal if she tells people?"

Luis sighed. "Look at this." He pointed at the pale pupil of his left eye. "Disgusting, right? One day when I was eight, my mother takes me to the Fulton Fish Market with her. She's buying some soft-shell crabs—bargaining with the fish guy, really getting into it because she loved to haggle—and I see this guy carrying an armful of gory sealskins. He sees me looking and grins real big. His teeth are like a shark's: tiny, sharp, and set too far apart."

Val clutched the banister, paint flaking under her fingernails.

"'You can see me?' he asks, and because I'm a dumb kid, I nod. My mother is right next to me, but she doesn't notice anything. 'Do you see me with both eyes?' he wants to know. I'm nervous now and that's the only thing that keeps me from telling him the truth. I point to my right eye. He drops the skins and they make a horrible, wet sound, falling all together like that."

holly black

Wax dripped down the side of the candle and onto Luis's thumb, but he didn't flinch or change the way he held it. More wax followed, forming a steady drip onto the stairs. "The guy grabs me by the arm and pushes his thumb into my eye. His face doesn't change at all while he's doing it. It hurts so bad and I'm screaming and that's when my mother finally turns around, finally sees me. And do you know what she and the soft-shell crab guy decide? That I scratched my own fucking eye somehow. That I ran into something. That I blinded myself."

The hair was standing up along Val's arms and she had that chill running down her spine, the one that told her just how freaked out she really was. She thought about the sealskins in his story, about the mermaid body she'd seen by the river, and came to no conclusions, except that there was no escape from horrible things. "Why are you telling me this?"

"Because it sucks to be me," Luis said. "One wrong step and they decide I don't need my other eye. That's what the big deal is.

"Dave and Lolli don't get it." His voice dropped to a whisper and he leaned close to her. "They're playing around with that drug, stealing from Ravus when I'm supposed to be repaying a debt.

Then they bring you in." He stopped, but she saw the panic in his eyes. "You're stirring shit up. Lolli is getting worse instead of better."

The troll appeared at the top of the ledge and looked down at Val. His voice was low and deep as a drum. "I cannot think what it was you came back for. Is there something you require?"

"The last delivery," she said. "It was a . . . mermaid? She's dead."

He went quiet, stared.

Val swallowed. "She looks like she's been dead awhile."

Ravus started down the stairs, frockcoat billowing. "Show me." His features changed as he got closer, the green of his skin fading, his features shifting until he looked human, like a gawky boy only a little older than Luis, a boy with odd, golden eyes and shaggy black hair.

"You didn't change your—," Val said.

"That's the way glamour is," said Ravus, cutting her off. "There's always some hint of what you were. Feet turned backward, a tail, a hollow back. Some clue to your true nature."

"I'll just get out of here," Luis said. "I was on my way anyhow."

"Luis and I have had an interesting conversation about you and the manner of our meeting," said the troll. It was disorienting to hear that deep, rich voice come from a young man.

"Yeah," Luis said, with a half-smile. "He conversed. I groveled."

That made Ravus smile in turn, but even as a man, his teeth looked a touch too long at the incisors. "I think this death concerns you too, Luis. Put off sleep a little longer and let's see what we might learn."

The only sounds on the waterfront came from waves lapping against the stones at the edge of the shore when Ravus, Val, and Luis arrived. The body was still there, hair flowing like seagrass, necklaces of shell and pearl and sand-dollar doves caught around her neck like strangling ropes, white face looking like a reflection of the moon on the water. Tiny fish darted around her, swimming in and out between her parted lips.

Ravus knelt down, cupped the back of the mermaid's skull in long fingers, and lifted up her head. Her mouth opened farther, showing thin, translucent teeth that looked like they might be made from cartilage. Ravus brought his face so close to the mermaid's that, for a moment, it looked like he might kiss her. Instead he sniffed twice before gently lowering her back into the water.

He looked at Luis with shadowed eyes, then shouldered off his frockcoat and spread it on the ground. He turned to Val. "If you take her tail, we can move her onto the cloth. I need to get her back to my workroom."

"Was she poisoned?" Luis asked. "Do you know what killed her?"

"I have a theory," said Ravus. He pushed back his hair with a wet hand, then waded into the East River.

"I'll help," Luis said, starting forward.

Ravus shook his head. "You can't. All that iron you insist on wearing could burn her skin. I don't want the evidence contaminated more than it has to be."

"The iron keeps me safe," Luis said, touching his lip ring. "Safer, anyway."

Ravus smiled. "At the very least, it is going to keep you safe from a repugnant task."

Val waded into the water and lifted the slippery tail, its ends as ragged as torn cloth. The scales glittered like liquid silver as they flaked off on Val's hand. There were patches of pale flesh exposed along the mermaid's side, where crabs had already started to feed on her.

"What a petty drama to watch play out," said a

voice coming from the mounds.

"Greyan." Ravus looked toward the shadows.

Val recognized the creature that came forward, the mannequin maker with the greening beard. But behind him were other folk she didn't know, faeries with long arms and blackened hands, with eyes like birds, faces like cats, tattered wings that were as thin as smoke and as bright as the neon lights from a distant bar sign.

"Another death," one of them said, and there was a low murmur.

"What is it that you are delivering this time?" Greyan asked. There was a burst of uncomfortable laughter.

"I came to discover what I could," said Ravus. He nodded to Val. Together, they moved the body onto the coat. Val felt nauseated as she realized that the fishy smell was coming from the flesh in her hands.

Greyan took a step forward, his horns white in the streetlight. "And look what is discovered."

"What are you implying?" Ravus demanded. In his human guise, he looked thin and tall, and beside Greyan's bulk, terribly outmatched.

"Do you deny you are a murderer?"

"Stop," said one of the others, a voice in shadow

attached to what appeared to be a long and spindly body. "We know him. He has made harmless potions for us all."

"Do we know him?" Greyan moved closer and from the folds of his cracked leather coat pulled out two short, curved sickles with dark bronze blades. He crossed them over his chest like an entombed pharaoh. "He went into exile because of a murder."

"Have a care," said a tiny creature. "Would you have all of us be judged now by the reason for our exile?"

"You know that I cannot refute the charge of murderer," Ravus said. "Just as *I know* it is cowardly to wave a sword at someone who has sworn not to swing a blade again."

"Fancy words. You think you're still a courtier," Greyan said. "But your clever tongue won't help you."

One of the creatures smirked at Val. It had eyes like a parrot and a mouth full of jagged teeth. Val reached around and picked up a length of pipe from the rocks. It felt so cold that it burned her fingers.

Ravus held up his hands to Greyan. "I don't wish to fight you."

"Then that's your ruin." He swung one sickle at Ravus.

holly black

The troll dodged the blade and ripped a sword out of the hand of another faerie, his fist wrapping around the sharp metal. Red blood ran from his palm. His mouth curled with something like pleasure and his glamour slipped away as though it was forgotten.

"You need what I make," Ravus spat. Fury twisted his face, making his features dreadful, forcing his fangs to bite into the flesh of his upper lip. He licked away the blood and his eyes seemed as full of glee as they were of rage. He tightened his grip on the blade of the sword, even as it bit deeper into his skin. "I give it freely, but were I the poisoner, were it my whim to kill one of the hundred I help, you would still have to live at my indulgence."

"I will live at no one's indulgence." Greyan swept his sickles toward Ravus.

Ravus swung the hilt of the sword, blocking the strike. The two circled each other, trading blows. Ravus's weapon was unbalanced by being held backward, and slippery with his own blood. Greyan struck quickly with his short bronze sickles, but each time Ravus parried.

"Enough," shouted Greyan.

A faerie with a long and looping tail rushed forward, gripping one of Ravus's arms. Another stepped up holding a silver knife in the shape of a leaf.

Just then Greyan swung at Ravus's wrist and Val moved before she knew she was moving. Instinct took over. All the lacrosse practices and video games came together somehow, and she swung the pipe at Greyan's side. It hit with a soft, fleshy sizzle, throwing him off balance for a moment. Then he wheeled toward her, both sickles hurtling down. Val barely had time to raise the pipe and brace herself before they hit, making the metal spark. She twisted to the side and Greyan stared at her in amazement before slamming the bronze blades into her leg.

Val felt cold all over and the background noises faded to a rushing in her ears. Her leg didn't even really hurt that much, although blood was soaking through her already-ripped pants.

In Val's other life, the one where she'd been almost a jock and didn't believe in faeries, she and Tom had played video games and fooled around in the finished basement of his house after school. Her favorite game was *Avenging Souls*. Her character, Akara, had a curved scimitar, a power move that let her chop off the heads of three of her opponents at once, and lots of health points. You could see them at the top of the screen, blue orbs that would turn to red with a popping noise the more wounded Akara got. That's all that happened. Akara didn't slow down when she got hurt, didn't stumble, scream, or faint.

Val did all those things.

Someone gripped Val's arm too tightly. She could feel nails against her skin. It hurt. Everything hurt. Val opened her eyes.

A young man was standing over her and at first she didn't know him. She pulled back, scuttling away from him. Then she saw the inky black hair and the swollen lips and the gold-flecked eyes. Luis stood in the background.

"Val," Luis said. "It's Ravus. Ravus."

"Don't touch me," said Val, wanting the pain to stop.

A bitter smile touched his mouth as his hands left her. "You could have died," Ravus said quietly.

Val took that as an encouraging sign that she wasn't actually dying.

Val woke, warm and sleepy. For a moment, she thought that she was back in her own bed, back at home. She wondered if she'd overslept and was missing school. Then she thought that maybe she'd been sick, but when she opened her eyes, she saw the flickering candlelight and the shadowy roof far above her. She was wrapped in a cocoon of lavender-scented blankets on top of a pile of cushions and rugs. Overhead the steady roar of traffic sounded almost like rain.

Val propped herself up on her elbow. Ravus was standing behind his worktable, chopping a block of some dark substance. She watched him for a moment, watched his long, efficient fingers cradling the knife, then she swung out one leg from under the covers. It was bare and bandaged at the thigh, wrapped with leaves and oddly numb.

He glanced over at her. "You're awake."

She flushed, embarrassed that he must have taken off her pants and that they'd been filthy. "Where's Luis?"

"He went back to the tunnels. I'm making you a draught. Do you think you can drink it?"

Val nodded. "Is it some kind of potion?"

He snorted. "It's naught but cocoa."

"Oh," Val said, feeling foolish. She looked over at him again. "Your hand isn't bandaged."

Ravus held it up, the palm unscarred. "Trolls heal fast. I'm hard to kill, Val."

She looked at his hand, at the table of ingredients, and shook her head. "How does it work, the

holly black

magic? How do you take ordinary things and make them magical?"

He looked at her sharply and then resumed chopping at the brown bar. "Is that what you think I do?"

"Isn't it?"

"I don't make things magical," he said. "I could, perhaps, but not in any quantity or potency. It would be beyond me, beyond almost anyone save a high Lord or Lady of Faerie. These things . . ." His hand swept over the worktable, over the hardened nuggets of chewed gum, the various wrappers and cans, the lipstick-stained butts of cigarettes. "Are already magical. People have made them so." He picked up a silvery gum wrapper. "A mirror that never cracks." He picked up a tissue with a blotted lipstick mouth on it. "A kiss that never ends." A cigarette. "The breath of a man."

"But mirrors and kisses aren't magical either."

At that he laughed. "So you don't believe a kiss is efficacious in transforming a beast or waking the dead?"

"And I'm wrong?"

"No," he said, characteristically wry. "You're quite correct. But, luckily, this potion is intended to do neither of those things."

She smiled at that. She thought about the way

she noticed all his glances, his sighs, the subtle changes in his face. She thought about what it might mean and she worried.

"Why do you always look like you do?" she asked. "You could look like anything. Anyone."

Ravus put down his mortar with a scowl and walked around the table. She felt a thrill run through her that was only part terror.

She was very conscious of lying in what must be his bed, but she didn't want to get out without any pants on.

"Ah, you mean with glamour?" He hesitated. "Make myself look less terrifying? Less hideous?"

"You're not—," Val began, but he held up his hand and she stopped.

"My mother was very beautiful. Doubtless, I have a broader idea of beauty than you do."

Val said nothing, nodding. She didn't want to think too closely about whether she had a broad idea of beauty. She'd always thought that she had a fairly narrow one, one that included her mother and other people who tried too hard. She'd always been a little contemptuous of beauty, as though it was something you had to trade away some other vital thing for.

"She had icicles in her hair," he continued. "It got so cold that frost would form, clumping her

holly black

braids together into crystalline jewels that would clatter together when she moved. You should have seen her in the candlelight. It lit up that ice like it was made of fire. It's a good thing she couldn't stand in the sunlight—she would have lit up the sky."

"Why couldn't she stand in the sunlight?"

"None of my people can. We turn to stone in the sun—and stay that way until nightfall."

"Does it hurt?"

He shook his head, but didn't answer. "Despite all that beauty, my mother never showed her true self to my father. He was mortal, like you, and around him, she always wore a glamour. Oh, she was beautiful glamoured, too, but it was a muted beauty. My brothers and sisters—we had to wear it, too."

"He was mortal?"

"Mortal. Gone in one faerie sigh. That's what my mother used to say."

"So you're . . . ?"

"A troll. Faerie blood breeds true."

"Did he know what she was?"

"He pretended not to know what any of us were, but he must have guessed. At the very least, he must have suspected we weren't human. He had a mill that sawed and dried wood from the several hundred acres of trees that he owned. Ash, aspen, birch, oak, willow. Juniper, pine, yew.

"My father had another family in the city, but my mother pretended to know nothing about that. There was a great deal of pretending. She made sure all my father's timber was fine and flat. It was beautifully planed and would neither warp nor rot.

"Faeries—we do nothing in moderation. When we love, we are all love. So was my mother. But in return she asked that he ring a bell at the top of the hill to let her know he was coming.

"One day my father forgot to ring the bell." The troll got up and walked over to the boiling milk and poured it into a Chinese cup. The smell of cinnamon and chocolate wafted toward her.

"He saw us all as we really were." Ravus sat beside her, long black coat pooling on the floor. "And fled, never to return."

She took the cup from him and took a cautious sip. It was too hot and burned her tongue. "What happened then?"

"Most people would be content for the story to end there. What happened then is that all my mother's love turned to hate. Even her children were nothing to her after that, just reminders of him." Val thought about her own mom and how she'd never questioned that she loved her. Of course she loved her mother—but now Val hated her. It didn't seem right that one could so easily become another.

"Her vengeance was terrible." Ravus looked at his hands and Val remembered the way he'd sliced them open holding a sword by its blade. She wondered if his rage was so great that he hadn't noticed the pain. She wondered if he loved the way his mother did.

"My mother was very beautiful, too," said Val. She wanted to speak again, but the single sip of the hot chocolate had filled her with such a delicious languor that she found herself slipping down into sleep once more.

Val woke to voices. The goat-hooved woman was there, speaking softly to Ravus.

"A stray dog, I might understand," she said. "But this? You are too softhearted."

"No, Mabry," Ravus said. "I am not." He looked in Val's direction. "I think she wants to die."

"Maybe you can help her after all," Mabry said. "You're good at helping people die."

"Have you come here for any purpose other than to smear me with my own filth?" he asked.

"That would be purpose enough, but there's

been another death," Mabry said. "One of the merfolk in the East River. A human found her body, but enough of it had been eaten by crabs that I doubt there will be much scandal."

"I know that," Ravus said.

"You know too much. You knew all of them. Every single one that has died," Mabry said. "Are you the murderer?"

"No," he said. "All the dead are exiles from the Seelie Court. Surely someone has noticed that."

"All poisoned," Mabry said. "That's what's being noticed."

Ravus nodded. "The scent of rat poison was on the mermaid's breath."

Val muffled a gasp, smothering her face with the blankets.

"Folk hold you responsible," Mabry said. "It is too like coincidence for all the dead to be your customers and to die within hours of getting a delivery from one of your human couriers."

"After the tithe failed in the Dark Court, dozens of Unseelie solitary fey must have left Nicnevin's lands. I don't see why anyone would think it more likely that I turned poisoner."

"Lord Roiben's lands now." Mabry's voice was full of something Val couldn't identify. "For as long as Silarial lets him keep them."

holly black

Ravus sniffed and Val thought she could see something in him that she hadn't before. He was dressed in a frockcoat, but one that was too new to be from the period it depicted. It was a costume, she realized, and was suddenly sure that Ravus was much younger than she'd assumed. She didn't know how faeries aged, but she thought that he was trying too hard to be sophisticated in front of Mabry. "I don't care who the Lord or Lady of the Dark Court is at the moment," he said. "May they all murder each other so we don't have to contend with them."

Mabry looked at him darkly. "I don't doubt that you wish that."

"I am going to send a message to the Lady Silarial. I know that she ignores the Folk so near the cities, but even she could not be indifferent to the murder of Bright Court exiles. We are still within her lands."

"No," Mabry said quickly, her tone different. "I think that would be unwise. To invoke the gentry might make things worse."

Ravus sighed and looked over at where Val was lying. "I find that difficult to imagine."

"Wait another little while before you send any messages," Mabry said.

He sighed. "It was kind of you to give me a warning, whatever you think of me."

"Warning? I just came to gloat," she said and swept out of the room, hooves clattering down the steps.

Ravus turned to Val. "You can stop pretending to be asleep now."

Val sat up, frowning.

"You think that she's unkind," said Ravus, standing with his back to her. Val wished she could see the expression on his face; his voice was difficult to interpret. "But it is my fault that she's trapped here in this city of stinking iron and she has other, even better reasons to hate me."

"What reasons?"

Ravus waved his hand above a candle and out of the smoke formed a young man's face, too lovely to be human. "Tamson," Ravus said. Pale gold hair dusted the figure's neck, blown back from his face, and as carelessly arranged as his smile.

Val gasped. She had never seen glamour used this way before.

The rest of Tamson formed out of nothingness, wearing armor that looked like it was made from bark, rough and dotted with moss. The glass sword was strapped to his side and, on him, it looked liquid, like water forced to hold an unlikely shape.

"He was my first and best friend in the Bright Court. He didn't care that I couldn't abide the sun.

He would visit me in darkness and tell me funny stories about what happened throughout the day." Ravus frowned. "I wonder that I was any good company."

"So the glass sword was his?"

"It is too slender a thing for me," Ravus said. Next to Tamson, another misty figure appeared, this one familiar to Val, although it took a moment to identify her. The faerie woman's brown hair was threaded with green, like the leafy carpet of a wood, and under the sweep of her red gown were goat's feet. She was singing a ballad, her rich, throaty voice thickening the words with promise. The troll gestured toward her. "Mabry, Tamson's lover."

"Was she your friend, too?"

"She tried to be, I think, but I was hard to look at." The glamoured Tamson put his hand on Mabry's arm and she turned toward him, song interrupted by their embrace. Over her shoulder, the smoky image of Tamson stared at Ravus, eyes burning like coals.

"He talked about her endlessly." Ravus's smile quirked his mouth.

The glamoured Tamson spoke. "Her hair is the color of wheat in high summer, her skin the color of bone, her lips red as pomegranates."

Val wondered if Ravus thought those descriptions

were accurate. She bit the inside of her cheek.

"He wanted to impress her," Ravus said. "He asked me to partner him so that he could show off his skill at dueling. I'm tall and I suppose I can look fierce.

"The Queen of the Bright Court likes fighting best of all the sports. She would organize tournaments where the Folk could show off their skill. I was new to the court and I did not much like to compete. My delights came in my work, my alchemy.

"It was a hot night; I remember that. I was thinking of Iceland, of the cool forests of my youth. Mabry and Tamson had been hissing words back and forth. I heard him say 'I saw you with him.'

"I wish I knew what it was Tamson saw, although I can guess." Ravus turned toward the cloaked windows. "The Folk do nothing by halves, we can be capricious. Each emotion is a draught that we must drain to the bottom, but sometimes I think we love the sour as much as the sweet. There is no sense in the Bright Court that because Mabry had dallied with Tamson and he loved her that she ought not dally with another."

"Tamson's armor was formed from bark, magicked to be harder than iron." He stopped speaking, closed his eyes and started up again. "He was a better swordsman than I, but he was distracted and I struck first. The sword, it cut through the bark like it was paper."

She saw the blow fall in the glamoured candle smoke. The armor crumbled around the blade, Tamson's look of surprise, Mabry's scream cutting through the air, high and sharp as though she'd realized what had happened a moment before anyone else had. Even the glamoured sound of it carried through the dusty room.

"When I fight, I fight like a troll—fury overtakes me. Perhaps another could have checked his blow; I could not. I still held the hilt of my sword, as though it was welded to my hand and impossible to let go. The blade looked like it had been painted red.

"Why would he take the magics off his own armor?" Ravus looked at her, and for a moment she thought he might be waiting for an answer. His gaze slid from her to look out at nothing and the glamour dispersed. "And yet he must have. No one else had any reason to wish him ill." Ravus's voice was low and harsh. "I knew he was in distress—I could see it on his face. I thought it would pass as all things passed . . . and selfishly, I was glad that Mabry had disappointed him. I had missed his companionship. I thought he would be mine again. He must have seen that vulgarity in me—why else would he choose me as the vehicle for his death?"

Val didn't know what to say. She composed sentences in her head: *It wasn't your fault. Everyone thinks terrible, selfish things. It had to have been an accident.* None of them seemed to mean anything. They were just words to fill silence. When he began speaking again, she realized how long she must have been quietly debating.

"Death is in poor taste in Faerie." He laughed mirthlessly. "When I said I would come to the city, go into exile here after Tamson's death, it suited them to let me. They didn't so much blame me for the death, as thought me tainted by it.

"Silarial, the Bright Court's Queen, commanded Mabry to accompany me so that we might grieve together. The stench of death clung to her, too, and made the other folk restive. So, she had to accompany me, the murderer of her lover, and here she must stay until I complete the term of my self-exile or I die."

"That's awful," Val said and at his silence realized how stupid and inadequate her words were. "I mean, obviously it's awful, but what I was thinking of was the part about sending her along with you. That's cruel."

He snorted, almost a laugh. "I would cut my own heart out to have Tamson's beating once more in his chest. Even for a moment. No sentence would have bothered me. But to have punishment and exile heaped on top of grief must have been almost too much for her to bear."

"What's it like here? I mean, to be in exile in the city?"

"I find it difficult. I am constantly distracted by the press of smells, the noise. There is poison everywhere, and iron so close that it makes my skin itch and my throat burn. I can only imagine how Mabry feels."

She reached one hand toward him and he took it, running his fingers over her calluses. She looked up into his face, trying to convey her sympathy, but he was looking intently at her hand.

"What are these from?" he demanded.

"What?"

"Your hands are rough," he said. "Calloused."

"Lacrosse," she said.

He nodded, but she could tell from his face that he didn't understand her. She might have said anything and he would have nodded that way.

"You have a knight's hands," he said finally, and let go of her.

Val rubbed her skin, not sure if she was trying to erase the memory of his touch or to recall it.

"It's not safe for you to keep doing deliveries." Ravus went to one of his cabinets and took out a jar where a butterfly fluttered. Then he pulled out a tiny scroll of paper and began to write in miniature script. "I owe you a greater debt than I can easily repay, but at least I can cancel your promise of servitude."

She looked toward the wall where the glass sword hung glimmering in the gloom, nearly as dark as the wall behind it. She remembered the feeling of the pipe in her hand, the adrenaline rush and clarity of purpose that she felt on the lacrosse field or in a fistfight.

"I want to keep doing deliveries for you," Val said. "There is something you could do to repay me, though, but you might not want to do it. Teach me how to use the sword."

He looked up from where he was rolling the scroll and attaching it to the leg of the butterfly. "Knowing it has caused me little joy."

She waited, not speaking. He hadn't said no.

He finished his work and blew, setting the little insect into the air. It flew a little unsteadily, perhaps

holly black

unbalanced by the slip of paper. "You want to kill someone? Who? Greyan? Perhaps you want to die?"

Val shook her head. "I just want to know how. I want to be able to do it."

He nodded slowly. "As you wish. It is your debt to dismiss and your right to ask."

"So you'll teach me?" Val asked.

Ravus nodded again. "I will make you as terrible as you desire."

"I don't want to be—," she started, but he held up his hand.

"I know you're very brave," he said.

"Or stupid."

"*And* stupid. Brave *and* stupid." Ravus smiled, but then his smile sagged. "But nothing can stop you from being terrible once you've learned how."

Chapter 8

Black milk of daybreak we drink you at night
we drink you at morning and midday we drink you at
  evening
we drink and we drink
                    —PAUL CELAN, "DEATH FUGUE"

Dave and Lolli and Luis sat on a blanket in the concrete park, some of Dave's finds spread out in front of them. Cardboard stuck out from underneath the cloth where it had been used as a liner between them and the cold that seeped up from the sidewalk. Dave's head was tilted back into Lolli's lap as she rolled his dreads in her palms, twisting and rubbing the roots. Lolli paused, picking something out of his hair, pinching it between her nails and slicking her fingers with wax from the tin beside her leg. Dave's eyes opened; then he closed them again in something like rapture.

Lolli's flip-flop–covered foot, splotchy and red with cold, stroked one of Luis's thighs. A book was open in front of him, and he squinted at it in the dimming light.

"Hey, guys," Val said, feeling shy as she walked up to them, as though being away for two or three days made her a stranger again.

"Val!" Lolli slid out from under Dave, leaving him to twist onto his elbows to avoid his head hitting the pavement. She ran over to Val, throwing her arms around her.

"Hey, my hair!" Dave yelled.

Val embraced Lolli, smelling unwashed clothes and sweat and cigarettes, and felt relief wash over her.

"Luis told us what happened. You're *crazy*." Lolli smiled, as though that was great praise.

Val's gaze skated to Luis, who looked up from his book with a grin that made his face seem handsome. He shook his head. "She is crazy. Head to head with a fucking ogre. Loony Lolli, Sketchy Dave, Crazy Val. You're all a bunch of freaks."

Val made a formal bow, dipping her head in their direction, and then sat on the blanket.

"Loony Luis, more likely," Lolli said, kicking her flip-flop in his direction.

"Luis One-Eye," Dave said.

Luis smirked. "Bug-head Dave."

"Princess Luis," Dave said. "Prince Valiant."

Val laughed, thinking of the first time Dave had called her that. "How about Dreaded Dave?"

Luis leaned over, grabbing his brother in a headlock, both of them rolling on the cloth, and said, "How about Baby Brother? Baby Brother Dave?"

"Hey," Lolli said. "What about me? I want to be a princess like Luis."

At that, the boys broke off, laughing. Val leaned back on the cloth and cardboard, the cold air pricking the hair along her arms, even under the coat. New Jersey seemed far away, and school an odd and nonsensical ritual. She smiled with contentment.

"Luis said that someone thinks we're poisoning faeries?" Lolli asked. She'd draped another blanket over her shoulders and reached for the hair wax.

"Or that Ravus is," Val said. "Ravus said something about stopping the deliveries. He thinks it might be too dangerous for us."

"Like he really cares," Luis said. "I bet he made a big, courtly show of thanks, but you're still a rat to him, Val. Just a rat that did a really good trick."

"I know that," Val lied.

"If he wants us to stop doing deliveries, it's to save his own ass." There was something in Luis's face as he said it, maybe the way he looked past her and off into nothingness, that made her wonder if he was wholly convinced himself.

"It had to be Ravus doing the poisoning," said Dave. "Getting us to do his dirty work. We don't know what we're carrying."

Val turned to look at him. "I don't think so. While I was staying there, that goat-footed woman—Mabry—came by. He said something to her about writing to the Seelie Queen. I guess if the Court's a gang, then the city is still somehow the Queen's turf. Anyway, why would he write to her if he was guilty?"

Dave sat upright, pulling his lock out of Lolli's fingers. "He's going to frame us. Luis just said it— we're all rats to them. When there's some problem, you just poison the rats and call it a day."

Val was uncomfortably reminded that it had been rat poison that killed the mermaid. Poison the rats. Rat poison. A glance at Luis showed him to be indifferent, however, biting a loose thread off his fingerless gloves.

Luis looked up and caught Val's eye, but there was nothing in his face, neither guilt nor innocence. "It is weird," he said. "With the shit you all shove up your noses and in your arms that you never hit any of the poison."

"You think I did it?" Lolli asked.

"You're the one who hates faeries," Dave said, speaking at the same time Lolli did so that their words overlapped. "You're the one who sees shit."

Luis held up his hands. "Wait a fucking minute. I don't think any of us poisoned any faeries. But I have to agree with Val. Ravus asked me a lot of questions the other night. He made me—" He scowled in Lolli's direction. "Some of it was about how you two wound up crawling around his place, but he asked me direct if I was the poisoner, if I knew who it was, if anyone had bribed me to do some sketched-out delivery. Why would he do all that if he took out those fey himself?"

Val nodded. Although the knowledge that rat poison had killed the faeries nagged at her, she remembered Luis's face inside the bridge. She believed that he'd been questioned thoroughly. Of course, maybe they were being set up, if not by Ravus, then by someone else. "What if something glamoured itself to look like one of us?"

"Why would it do that?" Lolli demanded.

"To make it seem like we're behind the deaths."

Luis nodded. "We should stop doing deliveries. Make whoever it is find some other suckers to frame."

Dave scratched his arm where the razor marks were. "We can't stop the deliveries."

holly black

"Don't be such a fucking junkie," said Luis.

"Val can get some Never, can't you, Val?" Lolli said with a sly look up through her pale lashes.

"What do you mean?" Val said, her voice sounding too defensive even to her own ears. She felt guilty, but she couldn't quite say why. She looked at Lolli's finger, as straight as if it had never been twisted out of its socket.

"The troll owes you, doesn't he?" Lolli's voice was pitched low, almost sensual.

"I guess." Val remembered the smell of the Never, Nevermore, burning on the spoon, and it filled her with longing. "But he paid his debt. He's going to show me how to use a sword."

"No shit?" Dave looked at her strangely.

"You should be careful," said Luis. Somehow, those words filled Val with an unease that had little to do with physical peril. She didn't meet Luis's eyes, staring instead at a mirror with a cracked frame on the blanket. Only moments earlier, she had felt great, but now unease had crept into her heart and settled there.

Lolli stood up suddenly. "Done," she pronounced, tousling Dave's locks so that they rustled like fat-bellied snakes. "Forget about all this. Time to play pretend."

"We don't have much left," Dave said, but he

was already standing up, already gathering the things from the blanket.

Together, the four of them crept back through the grate and into the tunnel.

Luis frowned as Lolli brought out the amber sand and her kit. "That isn't for mortals, you know. Not really."

In the near darkness, Dave brought a piece of foil to his nose, lighting beneath it so that the Never smoked. He took a deep sniff and looked solemnly at Lolli. "Just because something is a bad idea doesn't mean you can help doing it." His gaze traveled to Luis, and the look in his eyes made Val wonder what exactly it was he was thinking of.

"Give me some," Val said.

The days passed like a fever dream. During the day, Val did deliveries before going to Ravus's place inside the bridge, where he would show her swordplay in his shadowed rooms. Then at night, she shot her arms up with Never, and she and Dave and Lolli did whatever they pleased. They might sleep after or drink a little to ride out the hollowness that followed the high, when the world settled back into less magical patterns.

More and more, it was hard to remember the

holly black

basic things, like eating. Never made crusts of bread into banquet tables groaning with food, but no matter how much she ate, Val was always hungry.

"Show me how you hold a stick," Ravus said, during the first lesson. Val gripped the half broomstick like it was a lacrosse stick, both hands on it, separated by about a foot.

He slid her hands closer together and lower. "If you held a sword like that, you would cut your hand on the blade."

"Yeah, only an idiot would do that," Val said, just to see what he'd say.

Ravus didn't react with more than a quirk of his lip. "I know the weight feels off, but with a sword, it won't be. Here." He took down the glass sword and put it in her hand. "Feel the weight. See? It's balanced. That's the most important thing, balance."

"Balance," she repeated, letting the sword teeter in the palm of her hand.

"This is a pommel," he said, pointing to each place in turn. "This is the grip, the hilt, the cross-guard. When you hold the sword, the edge pointing to your opponent is the true edge. You want to hold the blade so that the point follows your opponent. Now stand like I'm standing."

She tried to copy him, legs apart and slightly bent, one foot in front of the other.

"Almost." He pushed her body into position, careless where he touched her. Her face heated when he pushed her thighs farther apart, but it embarrassed her more that only she seemed to notice his hands on her. To him, her body was a tool and nothing more.

"Now," he said, "show me how you breathe."

Sometimes Val and Dave and Luis and Lolli would talk about the strange things they'd seen or the creatures they'd spoken with. Dave told them about going all the way out to Brooklyn only to get chased through the park by a creature with short antlers growing from his brow. He'd screamed and run, dropping the bottle of whatever-it-was, and not looked back. Luis told them about running around town to find unsprayed flowers for a bogan that lived up near the Cloisters and had some kind of wooing planned. For his trouble, Luis had been given a bottle of wine that would never empty so long as you didn't look down the neck. It must have really been magic, too, not just glamour, because it worked, even for Luis.

"What else do they give you?" Val asked.

"Luck," Luis said. "And the means of breaking

holly black

faerie spells. My dad never did anything with his power. I'm going to be different."

"How do you break spells?" Val asked.

"Salt. Light. Eggshell soup. Depends on the spell." Luis took another pull from the bottle. He reached up to finger the metal bar that ran through his cheek. "But mostly iron."

There were no sword moves at the next practice, just stance and footwork. Back and forth across the dusty boards, keeping the half broomstick trained on Ravus as Val advanced and retreated. He corrected her when she took too large a step, when her balance was off, when her toe wasn't straight. She bit the inside of her cheek in frustration and continued moving, keeping the same distance between them, as though waiting for a battle that never began.

He turned suddenly to one side, forcing her to follow awkwardly. "Speed, timing, and balance. Those are the things that will make you into a competent fighter."

She gritted her teeth and stepped wrong again.

"Stop thinking," he said.

"I have to think," said Val. "You said I was supposed to concentrate."

"Thinking makes you slow. You need to move

as I move. Right now, you're merely following my lead."

"How can I know where you're going to go before you've gone there? That's stupid."

"It's no different from knowing where any opponent might move. How do you know where a ball is likely to go on the lacrosse field?"

"The only things you know about lacrosse are what I told you," Val said.

"I might say the same about you and sword fighting." He stopped. "There. You did it. You were so busy snapping at me that you didn't notice you were doing it."

Val frowned, too annoyed to be pleased, but too pleased to say anything more.

Lolli, Dave, and Val walked through the streets of the West Village, magicking fallen leaves into a slew of jeweled frogs that hopped in chaotic patterns, enchanting strangers to kiss, and otherwise making what trouble the three of them could imagine.

Val glanced across the street, through the gauzy drapes of a ground-floor apartment at a chandelier hung with carved monkeys and glittering with drops of crystal in the shape of tears.

"I want to go in there," Val said.

holly black

"Let's," said Lolli.

Dave walked up to the door and pressed on the bell. The intercom by the door buzzed to life and a garbled voice said something indecipherable.

"I'd like a cheeseburger," Dave said with a loud laugh, "a milk shake, and onion rings."

The voice spoke again, louder, but Val still couldn't understand the words.

"Here," she said, pushing Dave aside. She pressed the buzzer and held it until a middle-aged guy came to the door. He was wearing faded cords and a loose T-shirt that covered his slight paunch. Glasses rode low on his nose.

"What's your problem?" he demanded.

Val felt Never fizzing inside her arms, bursting like champagne bubbles. "I want to come in," she said.

The man's face went slack and he opened the door wider. Val smiled at him as she walked past and into his apartment.

The walls were painted yellow and hung with gilt-framed finger paintings. A woman was stretched out on the couch, holding a glass of wine. She started as Val came in, splashing her shirt with the red liquid. A little girl sat on a rug by the woman's feet, watching a program on the television that seemed to be about ninjas kicking each other. The little girl turned and smiled.

"This place is so nice," Lolli said from the doorway. "Who lives like this?"

"No one," said Dave. "They hire cleaners—maybe a decorator—to fake their life."

Val walked into the kitchen and opened the refrigerator. There were boxes of take-out, a few withered apples, and a carton of skim milk. She took a bite of the fruit. It was brown and mealy on the inside but still sweet. She couldn't understand why she'd never eaten a brown apple before.

Lolli picked up the bottle of wine from the coffee table and swigged from it, letting red juice run over her chin and cheeks.

Still eating the apple, Val walked to the couch where the woman sat numbly. The lovely apartment, with its stylish furniture and happy family, reminded Val of her dad's house. She didn't fit in here any more than she fit in there. She was too angry, too troubled, too sloppy.

And how was she supposed to tell her dad what had happened with Tom and her mom? It was like confessing to her father that she was bad in bed or something. But not telling him just let his new wife label her as Lifetime movie material, a troubled teen runaway in need of tough love. "See," Linda would say. "She's just like her mother."

holly black

"You never liked me," she told the woman on the couch.

"Yes," the woman repeated robotically. "I never liked you."

Dave pushed the man into a chair and turned to Lolli. "We could just make them leave," he said. "It would be so easy. We could live here."

Lolli sat down next to the little girl and plucked a ringlet of her dark hair. "What you watching?"

The girl shrugged.

"Would you like to come and play with us?"

"Sure," the little girl said. "This show is boring."

"Let's start with dress-up," Lolli said, leading the little girl into the back room.

Val turned to the man. He looked docile and happy in his chair, his attention wandering to the television.

"Where's your other daughter?" Val asked.

"I only have one," he said, with mild bafflement.

"You just want to forget about the other one. But she's still here."

"I have another daughter?"

Val sat down on the arm of his chair and leaned in close, her voice dropping to a whisper. "She's a symbol of the spectacular fuck-up that was your first marriage. Every time you see how big she is, you are reminded how old you are. She makes you feel vaguely guilty, like maybe you should know what sport she plays or what her best friend's name is. But you don't want to know those things. If you knew those things, you couldn't forget about her."

"Hey," Dave said, holding up a bottle of cognac that was mostly full. "Luis would like some of this."

Lolli walked back into the room wearing a leather jacket the color of burnt butter and a string of pearls. The little girl had a dozen glittering rhinestone pins in her hair.

"Are you happy at least?" Val asked the woman.

"I don't know," said the woman.

"How can you not know?" Val shouted. She picked up a chair and threw it at the television. The screen cracked and everyone jumped. "Are you happy?"

"I don't know," the woman said.

Val tipped over a bookcase, making the little girl scream. There were shouts outside the door.

Dave started laughing.

The light from the chandelier reflected in the crystals, sending shining sparks to glitter along the walls and ceilings. "Let's go," Val said. "They don't know anything."

holly black

• • •

The kitten wailed and wailed, pawing at Lolli with sharp little nails, jumping on her with its soft little body. "Shut up, Polly," she mumbled, rolling over and pulling the heavy blanket over her head.

"Maybe she's bored," Val said drowsily.

"It's hungry," Luis said. "Fucking feed it already."

Yowling, Polly jumped onto Lolli's shifting back, batting at her hair.

"Get off me," Lolli told the cat. "Go kill some rats. You're old enough to be on your own."

A shriek of metal grinding against metal and a dim light signaled the approach of a train. The rumbling drowned out the sound of the cat's cries.

At the last moment, as the whole platform was flooded with light, Lolli shoved Polly onto the tracks, right in front of the train. Val jumped up, but it was too late. The cat was gone and the metal body of the train thundered past.

"What the fuck did you do that for?" Luis shouted.

"She always pissed on everything anyway," Lolli said, curling up into a ball and closing her eyes.

Val looked over at Luis, but he just looked away.

• • •

After Ravus was satisfied with her stance, he taught her one move and made her repeat it until her limbs ached and she was convinced he thought she was stupid, until she was sure that he didn't know how to teach anyone anything. He taught her each move until it was automatic, as much a habit as biting the skin around her fingernails or the needle she shoved in her arm.

"Exhale," he shouted. "Time your exhalation to your strike."

She nodded and tried to remember to do it, tried to do everything.

Val liked Dumpster-diving with Sketchy Dave, liked walking through the streets, enjoyed the hunt and the occasional amazing find—like the stack of quilted blankets with silver lining that movers used to pad furniture, found piled up near a Dumpster, and which kept the four of them warm as mice even as November wore on, or the cool old rotary dial phone that someone paid ten bucks for. Most of the time, though, they were too dazed with Never to manage to make the old rounds. It was easier to take what they wanted anyway. All they had to do was ask.

A watch. A camera. A gold ring.

Those things sold better than a bunch of old crap anyway.

• • •

Then, finally, Ravus let her begin to put the moves together and spar. Ravus's longer arms put him at a continual advantage, but he didn't need it. He was pitiless, broomstick knocking her to the ground, driving her back against the walls, knocking over his own table when she tried to put it between them. Instinct and years of sports combined with desperation to let her get an occasional blow in.

When her stick struck his thigh, it was great to see the look on his face, rage that changed to surprise and then to pleasure in the space of a moment.

Backing off, they began again, circling each other. Ravus feinted and Val parried, but as she did, the room began to spin. She slumped against the wall.

His stick slammed into her other side. Pain made her gasp.

"What's wrong with you?" he shouted. "Why didn't you block the blow?"

Val forced herself to stand upright, digging her fingernails into her palm and biting the inside of her cheek. She was still dizzy, but she thought she might be able to pretend she wasn't. "I don't know. . . . My head."

Ravus swung the broomstick against the wall, splintering the wood and scratching the stone.

Dropping the remains of his stick, he turned back to her, black eyes hot as steel in a forge. "You should have never asked me to teach you! I can't restrain my blows. You'll be hurt by my hand."

She took an unsteady step back, watching the remains of the stick swim in her vision.

He took a deep, shuddering breath that seemed to calm him. "It might be the magic in the room that unbalanced you. I can often smell it on you, on your skin, in your hair. You're around it too much, perhaps."

Val shook her head and lifted her stick, assuming a starting position. "I'm okay now."

He looked at her, his face intense. "Is it the glamour that is making you weak or is it whatever you're doing out there on the street?"

"It doesn't matter," she said. "I want to fight."

"When I was a child," he said, making no move to change his stance, "my mother taught me how to fight with my hands before she let me use any kind of weapon. She and my brothers and sisters would beat me with brush, would pelt me with snow and ice until I fell into a rage and attacked. Pain was no excuse, nor illness. It was all supposed to feed my fury."

"I'm not making excuses."

"No, no," Ravus said. "That's not what I meant.

Sit down. Fury doesn't make you a great sword fighter; it makes you an unstable one. I should have seen that you were sick, but all I saw was a weakness. That is my flaw and I don't want it to be yours."

"I hate not being good at this," Val said as she flopped onto a stool.

"You are good. You hate not being great."

She laughed, but the sound came out sounding fake. She was upset that the world still wouldn't settle back into stillness and even more upset by his anger. "Why do you make potions when you had all that training to be a swordsman?"

He smiled. "After I left my mother's lands, I tried to leave the sword behind. I wanted to make something of my own."

She nodded.

"Although some among the Folk would be scandalized, I learned potion making from a human. She brewed cures, potions, and poultices for other mortals. You would suppose that people don't do that anymore, but in certain places, they do. She was always polite to me, a distant polite-ness as if she thought she was appeasing an uncer-tain spirit. I think she knew I wasn't mortal."

"But what about the Never?" Val asked.

"The what?"

She could see that he'd never heard it called that. She wondered if he had any idea what it could do for humans. Val shook her head, like she was trying to shake the words away. "The faerie magic. How did you learn what would make the potions magic?"

"Oh, that." He grinned in a way that was almost goofy. "I already knew the magic part."

In the tunnels, Val practiced the motion of a cut, the way she had to twist her hands as if she were wringing out a kitchen towel. She practiced the sweeping figure eight, turning the sword in her hands like girls flipped flags at game halftimes. Invisible opponents danced in the moving shadows, always faster and better balanced, with perfect timing.

She thought about lacrosse practice, drills of reverse-stick passes and sword dodges and change-of-hand dodges. She recalled learning to ball off the shaft of the stick, off the side wall, and catch the ball behind her back or between her legs.

She tried those moves with her half broomstick. Just to see if it could be done. Just to see if there was anything she could learn from it. She bounced a soda can off the makeshift hilt of her

holly black

stick, then kicked it with the side of her foot, sending it off at her shadow opponents.

Val looked at her face in a window as the rush hit. Her skin was like clay, endlessly malleable. She could change it into whatever she wanted, make her eyes big like an anime character, stretch her skin taunt across cheekbones sharp as knives.

Her forehead rippled, her mouth thinned, and her nose became long and looping. It was easy to make herself beautiful—she had gotten bored with that—but making herself grotesque was end- lessly interesting. There were just so many ways it could be done.

Val was playing a game she couldn't remember the name of, where you were trapped inside the necromancer's tower, running up endless stairs. Along the way, you picked up potions. Some of them made you smaller and some of them made you very tall so that you could fit through all the different doors. Somewhere there was an alchemist trapped very high up, so high that he couldn't see anything that was going on beneath him. Somewhere there was a monster, too, but sometimes the alchemist was the monster and the monster was the alchemist. She had a sword in her hand, but it didn't change when she did, so it was either a sharp toothpick in her palm or a huge thing she had to drag behind her.

When Val opened her eyes, she saw that she was lying on the sidewalk, her hips and back aching, her cheek patterned with concrete. People passed her in a steady stream. She'd missed practice again.

"What's wrong with that lady?" she heard a child's voice ask.

"She's just tired," a woman answered.

It was true; Val was tired. She closed her eyes and went back to the game. She had to find the monster.

Some afternoons she arrived at the bridge spent from the night before, glamour riot still licking at her veins, her eyes feeling charred around the edges as though they had been lined with ash, her mouth gone dry with a thirst she could not slake. She tried to hold her hands steady, to keep them from trembling and revealing her weakness. When she missed a blow, she tried to pretend that it was not because she was dizzy or sick.

"Are you unwell?" Ravus asked one morning when she was particularly shaky.

"I'm fine," Val lied. Her veins felt dry. She

holly black

could feel them pulse along her arms, the black sores on the insides of her elbows hard and hurting.

He perched on the edge of his worktable gesturing toward her face with his practice stick as though it were a wand. Val held up her hand automatically, but if he had been going to strike her she would have been much too late to stop the blow.

"You're observably pale. Your parries are dismal . . ." He let the sentence remain unfinished.

"I guess I'm a little tired."

"Even your lips are pallid," he said, outlining them in the air with the wooden blade. His gaze was intense, unflinching. She wanted to open her mouth and tell him everything, tell him about stealing the drug, about the glamour it gave them, about all the confused feelings that seemed to be canceling themselves out inside of her, but what she found herself doing was taking a step closer so that he had to stop gesturing and move the stick aside to keep from injuring her with it.

"I'm just cold," she said softly. She was always cold these days, but it was winter, so maybe that wasn't so strange.

"Cold?" Ravus echoed. He took her arm and rubbed it between his hands, watching them as though they were betraying him. "Better?" he asked warily.

His skin felt hot, even through the cloth of her shirt, and his touch was both soothing and electric. She leaned into him without thinking. His thighs parted, rough black cloth scratching against her jeans as she moved between his long legs.

His eyes were half-lidded as he pushed himself off the desk, their bodies sliding together, his hands still holding hers. Then, suddenly, he froze.

"Is something—," she started, but he pushed away from her abruptly.

"You should go," he said, walking to the window and then just standing there. She knew he dared not part the blinds while it was still day outside. "Come back when you are feeling improved. It does neither of us any good to practice when you're sickly. If you need something, I could—"

"I said I was fine." Val's voice pitched louder than she'd intended. She thought of her mother. Had she thrown herself at Tom like that? Had he turned away from her at first?

Ravus was still turned toward the window when she lifted an entire bottle of Never and put it in her backpack.

That night Lolli and Dave congratulated her on her score, shouting her name so loudly that people stopped on the grate above. Luis sat in shadows, chewing on his tongue ring and remaining silent.

That morning she collapsed onto her filthy mattress, like she did most mornings, and fell into a deep and dreamless sleep, as though she had never had any other life but this one.

Chapter 9

Those who restrain desire do so because theirs is weak enough to be restrained.

—William Blake, "The Marriage of Heaven and Hell"

Val woke up with someone pulling at the fastenings of her jeans. She could feel fingers at her waist, the twist and pinch of a button as it came undone.

"Get off me," she said, even before she realized it was Dave hunched over her. She twisted away from him and sat up, still flushed with the dregs of Never. Her skin was sweaty, even though cold air blew down from the grate above, and her mouth felt dry as sand.

"Come on," he whispered. "Please."

She looked down at her fingers and saw Lolli's chipped blue nail polish. Lolli's white boots were on her feet and she could see long faded blue locks of hair falling past her shoulders.

holly black

"I'm not her," she said, her voice thick with sleep and confusion.

"You could pretend," Sketchy Dave said. "And I could be anyone you wanted. Change me into anyone."

Val shook her head, realizing he'd glamoured her to be Lolli, wondering if he'd done it before with others, wondering if Lolli knew. The idea of playing at being other people was appalling, but with the remnants of Never still swarming inside of her, she was intrigued by the sheer wickedness of it. She felt the same thrill that had propelled her into the tunnels, the giddy pleasure of making a choice that is clearly, obviously wrong.

Anyone. She looked over at Lolli and Luis, sleeping close together but not touching. Val allowed herself to imagine Luis's face on Dave. It was easy; their faces weren't so different. Dave's expression shifted, taking on a bored and annoyed look that was all Luis.

"I knew you'd pick him," Dave said.

Val tilted her head forward and was surprised when hair fell to cover her face. She'd forgotten how shielded hair made her feel. "I didn't pick anyone."

"But you'll do it. You want to do it."

"Maybe." Val's mind made the figure above her

more familiar. Tom's stiff mohawk shone with hairspray and when he smiled, his cheeks dimpled. She could even smell the familiar scent of his patchouli aftershave. She leaned into it, flooded with a sense that she was back home and that none of this had ever happened.

The Tom above her sighed with what she thought might be relief and his hands moved under her shirt. "I knew you were lonely."

"I wasn't lonely," Val said automatically, pulling back. She didn't know if she was lying or not. Had she been lonely? She thought of faeries and their inability to lie and wondered what they did when they didn't know what the truth was.

At her thought of faeries, Tom's skin turned green, his hair blackened and fell around his shoulders until it was Ravus she saw, Ravus's long fingers that touched her skin and his hot eyes staring down at her.

She found herself frozen, repulsed by her own fascination. The tilt of his head was just right, his expression inquiring.

"You don't want me," she said, but whether she was speaking to the image of Ravus in front of her or to Dave, she wasn't sure.

He pressed his mouth against hers and she felt the sting of his teeth against her lip and she

holly black

shuddered with desire and with dread.

How could she not have known she wanted this, when now she wanted nothing else? She knew it wasn't really Ravus and that it was obscene to pretend it was, but she let him ease her jeans off her hips anyway. Her heart thudded against her chest, as though she'd been running, as though she was in some danger, but she reached up her arms and threaded her fingers through oil-black hair. His long body settled over hers and she gripped the muscles of his back, focusing on the hollow of his throat, the glittering gold of his slitted eyes, as she tried to ignore Dave's grunts. It was almost enough.

The next afternoon, as Ravus put Val through a series of sword moves holding the wooden blade, she watched his closed, remote face and despaired. Before, she had been able to convince herself that she didn't feel any way about him, but now she felt as if she'd had a taste of food that left her starving for a banquet that would never come.

Walking back from the bridge, she passed near where the Dragon Bus let off. Three hookers shivered in their short skirts. One girl in a faux ponyskin coat walked toward Val with a smile, then turned away as though she realized Val wasn't a boy.

At the next block, she crossed the street to avoid a bearded man in a miniskirt and floppy boots with their laces undone. Steam rose from under his skirt as he urinated on the sidewalk.

Val picked her way through the streets to the entrance to the tunnel platform. As she got close to the concrete park, she saw Lolli arguing with a girl wearing a monster-fur coat with a spiky rubber backpack over it. For a moment, Val felt an odd sense of disorientation. The girl was familiar, but so totally out of context that Val couldn't place her.

Lolli looked up. The girl turned and followed Lolli's glance. Her mouth opened in surprise. She started toward Val on platform boots, a sack of flour clutched in her arm. It was only when Val noticed someone had painted a face on the flour that she realized she was looking at Ruth.

"Val?" Ruth's arm twitched up like she was going to reach for Val, but then thought better of it. "Wow. Your hair. You should have told me you were going to cut it off. I would have helped you."

"How did you find me?" Val asked numbly.

"Your friend." Ruth looked back at Lolli skeptically. "She answered your phone."

Val reached automatically for her bag, even

knowing that her phone must not be inside of it. "I turned it off."

"I know. I tried to call you a zillion times and your voice mail is full. I've been freaking out."

Val nodded, at a loss as to what to say. She was conscious of the ground-in dirt on her pants, the black half-moons of her fingernails and the stink of her body, the smells that scrubbing in public rest rooms with your clothes mostly on didn't really make better.

"Listen," Ruth said. "I brought someone to meet you." She held out the sack of flour. It had eyes outlined with heavy black liner and a tiny, pursed mouth shaded with glittering blue nail polish. "Our baby. You know, it's hard on him with one of his mommies gone and it's hard on me, being a single parent. In Health class, I had to do all the worksheets alone." Ruth gave Val a wobbly smile. "I'm sorry I was such an asshole. I should have told you about Tom. I started to, like a million times. I just never got the words all of the way out."

"It doesn't matter anymore," Val said. "I don't care about Tom."

"Look," said Ruth. "It's freezing. Can we go inside? I saw a bubble tea place not too far from here."

Was it freezing? Val was so used to being cold when she wasn't using Never that it seemed normal for her fingers to be numb and her marrow to feel like it was made from ice. "Okay," she said.

Lolli had a smug expression on her face. She lit a cigarette and blew twin streams of white smoke from her nostrils. "I'll tell Dave you'll be back soon. I don't want him to worry about his new girlfriend."

"What?" For a moment, Val didn't know what she meant. Sleeping with Dave seemed so unreal, something done in the middle of the night, drunk with glamour and sleep.

"He says you two made it last night." Lolli sounded haughty, but Dave obviously hadn't told her that Val had looked like Lolli when she'd done it. It filled Val with a shameful relief.

Now Val understood why Ruth was here, why Lolli had lifted her cell phone and set up this scene. She was punishing Val.

Val guessed it was just about what she deserved. "It's no big deal. It was just something to do." Val paused. "He was just trying to make you jealous."

Lolli looked surprised and then suddenly awkward. "I just didn't think you liked him like that."

Val shrugged. "Be back in a while."

holly black

"Who is she?" Ruth asked as they walked toward the bubble tea place.

"Lolli," Val said. "She's okay, mostly. I'm crashing with her and some of her friends."

Ruth nodded. "You could come home, you know. You could stay with me."

"I don't think that your mom would be down with that." Val opened the wood and glass door and stepped into the smell of sugary milk. They sat at a table in the back, balancing on the small rosewood boxes the place had for seats. Ruth thrummed her fingers on the glass top of the table as though her nerves had settled into her skin.

The waitress came and they ordered black pearl tea, toast with condensed milk and coconut butter, and spring rolls. She stared at Val for a long moment before she left their table, as if evaluating whether or not they could pay.

Val took a deep breath and resisted the urge to bite the skin around her finger. "It's so weird that you're here."

"You look sick," Ruth said. "You're too skinny and your eyes are one big bruise."

"I—"

The waitress set their things down on the table, forestalling whatever Val had been about to say. Glad for the distraction, Val poked at her drink with the fat, blue straw, and then sucked up a large, sticky tapioca and a mouthful of sweet tea. Everything Val did seemed slow, her limbs so heavy that chewing on the tapioca felt exhausting.

"I know you're going to say that you're fine," Ruth said. "Just tell me that you really don't hate me."

Val felt something inside her waver and then she finally was able to start to explain. "I'm not mad at you anymore. I feel like such a sucker, though, and my mother . . . I just can't go back. At least not yet. Don't try to talk me into it."

"When then?" Ruth asked. "Where are you staying?"

Val just shook her head, putting another piece of toast in her mouth. They seemed to melt on her tongue, gone before she realized she'd eaten them all. At another table, a group of glitter-covered girls exploded in laughter. Two Indonesian men looked over at them, annoyed.

"So what did you name the kid?" Val asked.

"What?"

"Our flour baby. The one I ran off on without even paying child support."

Ruth grinned. "Sebastian. Like it?"

Val nodded.

"Well, here's something that you probably

won't like," Ruth said. "I'm not going home unless you come with me."

No matter what Val said, she couldn't talk Ruth into leaving. Finally, thinking that seeing the actual squat might convince her, Val brought her down to the abandoned platform. With someone else there, Val noticed anew the stink of the place, sweat and urine and burnt-sugar Never, the animal bones on the track and the mounds of clothes that never got moved because they were crawling with bugs. Lolli had her kit unrolled and was shaking some Never onto a spoon. Dave was already soaring, the smoke from his cigarette forming the shapes of cartoon characters that chased each other with hammers.

"You've got to be kidding me," Luis said. "Let me guess. Another stray cat for Lolli to shove off onto the tracks."

"V-val?" Ruth's voice trembled as she looked around.

"This is my best friend, Ruth," Val said before she realized how juvenile that sounded. "She came looking for me."

"I thought we were your best friends." Dave smiled a smile that was half-leer and Val regretted letting him touch her, letting him think he had some power over her.

"We're all best friends," Lolli said, shooting him a glare as she rested one of her leg's on Luis's, her boot nearly touching his crotch. "All the bestest of friends."

Dave's face crumpled.

"If you were any kind of friend to her, you wouldn't drag her into this shit," Luis told Val, twisting away from Lolli.

"How many people are down here? Come out where I can see you," a gruff voice called.

Two policemen walked down the stairs. Lolli froze, the spoon in her hand still over the fire. The drug started to blacken and burn. Dave laughed, a weird crazy laugh that went on and on.

Flashlights cut through the dim station. Lolli dropped her spoon, grown too hot to hold, and the beams converged on her, then moved to blind Val. She shaded her eyes with her hand.

"All of you." One of the cops was a woman, her face stern. "Stand against the wall, hands on your head."

One beam caught Luis and the male cop nudged him with his boot. "Go. Let's go. We heard some reports there were kids down here, but I didn't believe it."

Val stood slowly and walked to the wall, Ruth beside her. She felt so sick with guilt that she wanted to vomit. "I'm sorry," she whispered.

Dave just stood stock still in the middle of the platform. He was shaking.

"Something wrong?" the female cop shouted, making it not at all a question. "Against the wall!" With that, her speech turned to barking. Where she had stood was a black dog, larger than a Rottweiler, with foam running from its mouth.

"What the hell?" The other cop turned, pulled out his gun. "That your dog? Call it off."

"It's not our dog," Dave said with an eerie smile.

The dog turned toward Dave, growling and barking. Dave just laughed.

"Masollino?" the policeman yelled. "Masollino?"

"Stop fucking around," Luis called. "Dave, what are you doing?"

Ruth dropped her arms from her head. "What's going on?"

The dog's teeth were bright as it advanced against the policeman. He pointed the gun at it and the dog stopped. It whined and he hesitated. "Where's my partner?"

Lolli giggled and the man looked up sharply, then quickly back at the dog.

Val took a step forward, Ruth still holding her arm so tight that it hurt. "Dave," she hissed. "Come on. Let's go."

"Dave!" Luis yelled. "Turn her back!"

The dog moved at that, turning and leaping toward where they stood, lolling tongue a slash of red in the dark.

Two sharp pops were followed by silence. Val opened her eyes, not even aware she had closed them. Ruth screamed.

Lying on the ground was the female cop, bleeding from her neck and side. The other officer stared in horror at his own gun. Val froze, too stunned to move, her feet like lead. Her mind was still groping for a solution, some way to undo what had been done. *This is just an illusion,* she told herself. *Dave is playing a joke on all of us.*

Lolli jumped down into the well of the tracks and took off, gravel crunching under her boots. Luis grabbed Dave's arm and pulled him toward the tunnels. "We have to get out of here," he said.

The police officer looked up as Val leaped off the side of the platform, Ruth behind her. Luis and Dave were already disappearing into the darkness.

A shot rang out behind them. Val didn't look back. She ran along the track, clutching Ruth's hand like they were little kids crossing the road. Ruth squeezed twice, but Val could hear her start to sob.

holly black

"Cops never understand anything," Dave said as they moved through the tunnels. "They got all these quotas about arresting people and that's all they care about. They found our place and they were just going to lock it up so nobody could ever use it and where's the sense in that? We're not hurting anyone by being down there. It's our place. We found it."

"What are you talking about?" Luis said. "What were you thinking back there? Are you bug-fuck crazy?"

"It's not my fault," Dave said. "It's not your fault. It's not anybody's fault."

Val wished he would shut up.

"That's right," Luis said, his voice shaking. "It's nobody's fault."

They emerged in the Canal Street station, hopping on the platform and getting on the first train that stopped. The car was mostly empty, but they stood anyway, braced against the door as the train swayed along.

Ruth had stopped crying, but her makeup made dark smudges on her cheeks and her nose was red. Dave seemed emptied of all emotion, his eyes not meeting anyone else's. Val couldn't imagine what he was feeling at that moment. She wasn't even sure how to name what she felt.

"We can crash in the park tonight," Luis said. "Dave and I did that before we found the tunnel."

"I'm going to take Ruth to Penn Station," Val said suddenly. She thought of the policewoman, the memory of her death like a weight that got heavier with each step away from the corpse. She didn't want Ruth dragged down with the rest of them.

Luis nodded. "And you're going with her?"

Val hesitated.

"I'm not getting on that train alone," Ruth said fiercely.

"There's someone I have to say good-bye to," Val said. "I can't just disappear."

They got off at the next stop, transferred to an uptown train and rode to Penn Station, then walked upstairs to check the times. Afterward they settled in the Amtrak waiting area, and Lolli bought coffee and soup that none of them touched.

"Meet me here in an hour," Ruth said. "The train leaves fifteen minutes after that. You can say good-bye to this guy in that time, right?"

"If I'm not back, you have to get on the train," Val said. "Promise me."

Ruth nodded, her face pale. "So long as you promise to be back."

"We're going to be by the weather castle in

holly black

Central Park," Lolli said. "If you miss your train."

"I'm not going to miss it," Val said, glancing at Ruth.

Lolli swirled a spoon into a tub of soup, but didn't raise it to her mouth. "I know. I'm just saying."

Val stumbled out into the cold, glad to be away from them all.

When she got to the bridge, it was still light enough to see the East River, brown as coffee left too long on the burner. Her head hurt and the muscles in her arms spasmed and she realized that she hadn't had a dose of Never since the evening before.

Never more than two days in a row. She couldn't remember when that rule had been forgotten and the new rule had become every day and sometimes more than that.

Val knocked on the stump and slipped inside the bridge, but despite the threat of daylight, Ravus was gone. She considered finger painting a message on a torn grocery flier, but she was so tired that she decided to wait a little while longer. Sitting down in the club chair, the scents of old paper, leather, and fruit lulled her into leaning back her head and parting the curtain just slightly. She sat for an oblivious hour, watching the sun dip lower, setting the sky aflame, but Ravus didn't return and she only felt worse. Her muscles, which had ached like they did after exercise, now burned like a charley horse that woke you from sleep.

She looked through his bottles and potions and mixtures, careless of what she disturbed and where things were moved, but she found not a single granule of Never to take away the pain.

A family was finishing their picnic on the rocks as Val shuffled into Central Park, the mother packing up leftover sandwiches, a lanky daughter pushing one of her brothers. The two boys were twins, Val noticed. She'd always found twins sort of creepy, as though only one of them could be the real one. The father glanced at Val, but his eyes rested on a cyclist's long, bare legs as he slowly chewed his food.

Val walked on slowly, legs aching, past a lake thick with algae, where a riderless boat floated along in the dimming light. An older couple strolled by the bank, arm in arm, as a jogger in spandex huffed his way around them, mp3 player bobbing against his biceps. Normal people with normal problems.

The path continued over a courtyard whose walls were carved with berries and birds, vines so intricate they nearly looked alive, blooming roses, and less familiar flowers.

holly black

Val stopped to lean against a tree, its roots exposed and tangled like the pattern of veins under her skin, the pewter bark of the trunk wet and dark with frozen sap. She'd been walking for a while, but there was no castle in sight.

Three boys with low-slung pants passed, one bouncing a basketball off his friend's back.

"Where's the weather castle?" she called.

One boy shook his head. "No such thing."

"She means Belvedere Castle," said the other, pointing his hand at an angle, halfway back in the direction she'd come from. "Over the bridge and through the Ramble."

Val nodded. *Over the bridge and through the woods.* Everything hurt, but she kept going, anticipating the sting of the needle and the sweet relief it would bring. She thought back to Lolli sitting by the fire with the spoon in her hand, and her breath stopped at the thought that all the Never was still back there, in the tunnels, with the dead woman— then hated herself, that that was what she worried about, that that was what stopped her breath.

The Ramble was a maze of trails, crossing one another, trailing off into dead ends, and doubling back on themselves. Some paths appeared intentional, others seemed created by pedestrians sick of trying to pick their way through the fickle course. Val trudged along, crunching leaves and twigs, her hands in her pockets, gripping her skin through the thin backing of the coat as though digging fingers could punish her body into not hurting.

In the cover of the patchy branches, two men were twined together, one of them in a suit and overcoat, the other in jeans and denim jacket.

At the top of the hill was a large, gray castle with a spire that reached far above the tree line. It appeared to be a grand and ancient estate, rendered strange by being set against the shining lights of the city at dusk, a thing completely out of place. As Val walked closer, she saw that an array of taxidermied creatures were just inside the window, their black eyes watching her through the glass.

"Hey," a familiar voice called.

Val turned to see Ruth leaning up against a pillar. Before she could think of what to say, she noticed Luis stretched out against the landing that overlooked a lake and a baseball diamond, kissing Lolli with deep, wet, soft kisses.

"I knew you never intended to show up," Ruth said, shaking her head.

"You said that you would get on the train even

if I didn't," Val said, trying for self-righteous anger, but the words came out sounding lamely defensive.

Ruth crossed her arms over her chest. "Whatever."

"Where's Dave?" Val asked, looking around. The park was getting darker and she didn't see him anywhere close by.

Ruth shrugged and reached for a cup by her feet. "He went off to do some thinking or something. Luis went after him, but came back alone. I guess he's freaked out. Shit, I'm freaked out—that woman changed into a dog and now she's dead."

Val didn't know how to explain things so that Ruth would understand, especially because it would make everything so much worse. It was better to believe that the cop had turned into a dog than that she had been turned into one. "Dave's not going to be happy about that." Val gestured with her chin toward Lolli and Luis, ignoring the question of magic altogether.

Ruth grimaced. "It's disgusting. Those callous fuckers."

"I don't get it. All this time she's been after him and he picks now to get it on?" Val couldn't understand. Luis was an asshole, but he cared about his brother. It wasn't like him to leave Dave to wander around Central Park while he got it on with a girl.

Ruth frowned and held out the cup she was holding. "They're your friends. Here, have some tea. It's disgustingly sweet, but at least it's warm."

Val took a sip, letting the liquid warm her throat, trying to ignore the way her hand was shaking.

Luis pulled back from Lolli, and gave Val a lopsided grin. "Hey, when did you show up?"

"Do either you have any Never?" Val blurted. She didn't think she could stand the pain much longer. Even her jaw felt cramped.

Luis shook his head and looked at Lolli. "No," she said. "I dropped it. Did you get anything from Ravus?"

Val took a deep breath, trying not to panic. "He wasn't there."

"Did you see Dave on your way in?" Lolli asked.

Val shook her head.

"Let's go down to the crash spot," Luis said. "I think its dark enough to keep us hidden."

"Can Dave find us?" Ruth asked.

"Sure," Luis said. "He'll know where to look. We slept there before."

holly black

Val gritted her teeth in frustration, but she followed the others as they jumped the gate on one side of the castle and crept down the rocks beneath it. There was a shadowed plateau overhung enough by another boulder to give them a little shelter. Val noticed that they'd already loaded it up with some cardboard.

Luis sat down and Lolli leaned against him, eyes going half-lidded. "I'll scrounge up some better supplies tomorrow," he said, leaning down to press his mouth to hers.

Ruth put one arm around Val and sighed. "I can't believe this."

"Me either," Val said, because suddenly all of it seemed equally surreal, equally random and unbelievable. It felt less possible that Ruth should be sleeping on cardboard in Central Park than that faeries existed.

Luis slid his hands up under Lolli's skirt and Val took took another sip of the cooling tea, ignoring the flash of skin, the glimmer of steel rings, trying not to notice the wet sounds and the giggling. As she turned her head, she saw the leg of Luis's baggy pants, hiked up so high that the scorch marks on the inside of his knee were visible, scorch marks that could only come from Never.

As Ruth's breath evened out into sleep and Lolli and Luis's breath escalated into something else, Val bit the inside of her lip and rode out the pain of withdrawal.

Chapter 10

As the night wore on, Val got no better. The cramping of the muscles under her skin grew until she stood up and crept away from their crash spot so that she could at least twist and move as her discomfort urged. She walked across the rocks and started back through the Ramble, scattering a flurry of crumpled leaves from their branches. She took another sip of the tea, but it had turned icy cold.

Val had grown up thinking of Central Park as dangerous, even more than the rest of New York, the kind of place where perverts and murderers lurked behind every bush, just waiting for some innocent jogger. She remembered countless news stories about stabbings and muggings. But now the park just seemed tranquil.

She picked up a stick and did lunging drills, thrusting the tip of the wood into the knothole of a thick elm until she figured she'd cowed any squirrels that might have lived there. The movements made her feel dizzy and slightly nauseated and when she shook her head, she thought she saw moving lights on a nearby path.

The wind picked up just then and the air felt charged, the way it did before a thunderstorm, but when she looked again, she saw nothing. Scowling, she squatted down and waited to see if there was anyone there.

The wind whipped past her, nearly pulling her backpack off her shoulder. This time she was sure she heard laughter. She turned, but there were only the thick bands of ivy crawling up a nearby tree.

The next gust of wind hit her then, knocking the cup out of her hand, spilling the remains of the tea in a puddle and rolling the white cup in the wet dirt.

"Stop it!" Val yelled, but in the silence that followed, her words seemed futile, even dangerous to shout into the still air.

A whistle turned her head. There, sitting on a

holly black

stump, was a woman made entirely of ivy. "I smell glamour, thin as a dusting of snow. Are you one of us?"

"No," Val said. "I'm not a faerie."

The woman inclined her head in a slight bow.

"Wait. I need—," Val started, but she didn't know how to finish. She needed to score; she needed Never but she had no idea if the faeries had a name for it.

"One of the sweet tooths? Poor creature, you've wandered far from the revels." The ivy woman walked past Val and down toward the bridge. "I'll show you the way."

Val didn't know what the ivy woman meant, but she followed, not only because Lolli and Luis were breaking Dave's heart on some nearby rocks and she didn't want to have to see it, not just because the dead eyes of the policewoman seemed to follow her in the darkness, but because the only thing that seemed important right then was stopping her own pain. And where there were faerie revels, there would be some way to find surcease.

The ivy woman led Val back to the terrace with its carved walls of birds and branches, the fountain at its center, and the lake beyond. The faerie rustled across the tiles, a moving column of greenery. Fog rolled up off the water, a silvery mist that hung in the air for a moment before it roiled forward, too dense and fast to be natural. Val's skin prickled but she was too dazed and full of aches to do more than stumble back as the fog came in like the tide on some dark shore.

It settled around her, warm and heavy, carrying a strange perfume of rot and sweetness. Music ghosted through the air—the tinkling of bells, a moan, the shrill notes of a flute. Val walked unsteadily, engulfed and blinded by swells of mist. She heard a chorus of laughter, close by, and turned. The fog ebbed in places, leaving Val looking at a new landscape.

The terrace was still there, but the vines had grown from the stone into wild looping things, blooming with strange flowers and thorns long and thin as needles. Birds flew from their sculpted nests to pick at the swollen grapes that hung from the stair rails and squabble with fist-sized bees over the steely apples that littered the pier.

And, too, there were faeries. More than Val might have imagined could live among the iron and steel of the city, faeries with their strange eyes and knifelike ears, in skirts woven of nettle or meadowsweet, in T-shirts and vests with embroidered roses and in nothing at all, their skin gleaming under the moon. Val passed a creature with legs that seemed to be branches and a face carved from bark and a little man that peered at her through opera glasses with lenses of blue beach glass. She passed a man with spines that ran along his hunched back. He smelled of sandalwood and she thought she knew him. Each fey creature seemed bright as leaping flame and wild as wind. Their eyes glowed hot and terrible in the moonlight and Val found herself afraid.

And, too, along the edge of the lake were cloths woven with gold and heaped with all manner of delicacies. Dates, quinces, and persimmons lay on platters of cracked and dried leaves, next to decanters of sapphire and peridot wines. Cakes piled with roasted acorns were stacked beside spits of limp pigeons and cups of viscous syrups. Nearby them, in a heap, were Ravus's white apples, their red innards visible through vellum skin, promising Val respite from pain.

She forgot her fear.

She grabbed one, and bit into the warm, sweet flesh. It slid down her throat like a bloody chunk of meat. Fighting back nausea, she bit again and again, juice sluicing over her jaw, the skin of the fruit giving under her sharp teeth. It didn't feel like Never, but it was enough to numb her limbs and still her trembling.

Relieved, Val sank down by the lake as a creature of moss and lichen surfaced for a moment with a flailing pewter fish in her mouth, then dove again. Too tired to move and too relieved to be anything but sated, Val contented herself by watching the crowd. To her surprise, she saw that she was not the only human. A girl, too young to be out of middle school, rested her head in the lap of a blue faerie with black lips who braided tiny bells and beggarsweed into the child's pigtails. A man with graying hair and a tweed coat knelt beside a green girl with mossy, dripping hair. Two young men ate slivers of white apples off the edge of a blade, licking the knife to get all of the juice.

Were they the sweet tooths? Human thralls, willing to do anything for a taste of Never, not even knowing what it was to stick it in your arm or burn it up your nose. *Never,* Val told herself. *Never again Never. Never more. Never Never NeverNeverLand.* She didn't need to make the shadows dance. She didn't need to keep choosing the wrong path, gloating that at least she was picking her disaster. No matter how bad her decisions, they weren't keeping any other troubles at bay.

Another faerie came down the stairs. There was something wrong with his skin; it looked mottled and bubbling in places. One of his ears and part of his neck looked like they were sculpted crudely from clay. Some of the others drew back as he strode across the terrace.

"Iron sickness," someone said. Val turned to see one of the honey-haired faerie girls from Washington Square Park. Her feet were still bare, although she wore an anklet of holly berries.

Val shuddered. "Looks like he was burned."

"Some say that's going to happen to all of us if we don't stay in the park or go back where we came from."

"Were you exiled here?"

The faerie girl nodded. "One of my lovers was also the lover of a well-favored Lord. He made it appear as though I had stolen a bolt of cloth. It was magical fabric, the kind that shows you stories— precious stuff—and the punishment from the weaver was likely to be both elegant and severe. My sisters and I went into exile until we could prove my innocence. But what of you?"

Val had leaned forward, imagining the marvelous material, and was caught off guard by the faerie's question. "I guess you could say I was in exile." Then, looking around, she asked. "Is it always like this here? Do all the exiles come here every night?"

The honey-haired faerie laughed. "Oh, yes. If you have to go Ironside, at least you can come here. It's almost like being back at court. And, of course, there's gossip."

Val smiled. "What kind of gossip?" She was back to being a sidekick. It was automatic for her to ask the questions that her companion wanted to answer and a relief to listen. The faerie's words drowned out her own restless thoughts.

The girl grinned. "Well, the best bit of gossip is that the Bright Lady, the Seelie Queen Silarial, is here in the iron city. They say that she's to take care of the poisonings. Apparently Mabry—one of the exiled gentry—knows something. Everyone's heard they had a meeting."

Val sank her nails into the back of her other hand. Had Mabry accused Ravus? She thought of Ravus's abandoned place inside the bridge an scowled.

"Oh, look," the faerie whispered. "There she is. See how everyone hangs back, pretending they aren't dying to ask her to prove the rumors."

Val stood up. "I'll ask her."

Before the honey-haired faerie could protest or applaud, Val threaded her way through the Folk. Mabry wore a gown of palest cream, her green-and-brown hair piled up on her head with a comb

holly black

made from the inside of a shell. It looked strangely familiar to Val, but she couldn't place it.

"That's a pretty comb," she said, since she'd been staring at it.

Mabry drew it from her hair, letting the locks tumble down her back, and gave Val a wide, lush smile. "I know you. The servant Ravus has become overfond of. Take this little trinket if you like. Perhaps your hair will grow into it."

Val ran her fingers over the cool surface of the shell, but she was sure that a gift delivered with such a barb didn't deserve any thanks.

Mabry reached out a finger and touched the side of Val's mouth. "I see you've had a taste of what your skin has been drinking."

Val started. "How did you know?"

"It is my habit to know things," Mabry said, turning to walk off before Val got to ask a single thing she wanted to know.

Val tried to follow Mabry, but a faerie with hair of long weeds and a smile full of wicked laughter interposed himself. "My lovely, let me devour your beauty."

"You've got to be joking," Val said, trying to push past him.

"Not in the least," he said, and suddenly, strangely, Val could feel desire twist in her belly.

Her face went hot. "I can make even your dreams be of want."

A hand caught her throat and a deep, rough voice spoke low and close to her ear. "And now what is your training good for?"

"Ravus?" Val asked, although she knew his voice.

The other faerie slunk away, but Ravus kept his fingers at her neck. "It's dangerous here. You should be more careful. Now I'd like you to at least try and break free."

"You never taught me—," she began, but then she stopped, ashamed of the way her voice sounded like whining. He was teaching her now. After all, he was giving her time to think what the possible moves might be. It wasn't as though he was choking her. He was giving her time to win.

Val relaxed, pressing her back to his chest and grinding against him. Startled, he loosed his grasp and she pulled free. He clutched her arm, but she spun around and pressed her mouth to his.

His lips were rough, chapped. She felt the sting of fangs against her bottom lip. He made a sharp sound in the back of his throat and closed his eyes, mouth opening under hers. The smell of him—of cold, damp stone—made her head swim. One kiss slid into another and it was perfect, was exactly right, was real.

holly black

He pulled back abruptly, turning his head so that he wasn't looking at her. "Effective," he said.

"I thought maybe you wanted me to kiss you. Sometimes I thought I could see it." Her heart was thundering in her chest and her cheeks were scalding, but she was pleased that she sounded calm.

"I didn't want you . . . ," Ravus said. "I didn't want you to see it."

She almost laughed. "You look so shocked. Hasn't anyone ever kissed you before?" Val wanted to do it again, but she didn't dare.

His voice was cool. "On rare occasions."

"Did you like it?"

"Then or now?"

Val sucked in a breath, let it out with a sigh. "Both. Either."

"I liked it," he said softly. It was then that she remembered he could not lie.

She ran her hand over his cheek. "Kiss me back."

Ravus caught her fingers, clutched them so hard that they hurt. "Enough," he said. "Whatever game you are playing at, end it now."

She pulled her hand out of his grip, sobering abruptly, and took several steps back from him. "I'm sorry—I thought—" In truth, she couldn't recall what she'd thought, what had made this seem like a good idea.

"Come along," he said, not looking at her. "I'll take you back to the tunnels."

"No," Val said.

He stopped. "It would be unwise to remain here, no matter your—"

Val shook her head. "That's not what I mean. Someone found our place. There's nowhere to go back to." It had been a long time since there was something to go back to, anything to go back to anywhere.

He spread his hand as though trying to express something inexpressible. "We both know that I am a monster."

"You're not—"

"It demeans you to cover rotten meat with honey. I know what I am. What would you want with a monster?"

"Everything," Val said solemnly. "I'm sorry I kissed you—it was selfish and it upset you—but you can't ask me to pretend *I* didn't want to."

He regarded her warily as she took a step closer to him. "I'm not very good at explaining things," she said. "But I think you have beautiful eyes. I love the gold in them. I love that they're different from my eyes—I see mine all the time and I'm bored with them."

He snorted with amusement, but stayed still.

She reached up and touched the pale green of his cheek. "I like all the things that make you monstrous."

His long fingers threaded through the peach fuzz of her hair, clawed nails resting carefully against her skin. "I'm afraid that whatsoever I touch is spoilt by the contact."

"I'm not scared of being spoiled," Val said.

The side of Ravus's mouth twitched.

A woman's voice pierced through the air, sharp as the clang of a bell. "You sent for Silarial after all."

Val whirled. Mabry stood in the courtyard, tendrils of hair caught by the breeze. All around them, Folk were staring. After all, here was a chance for gossip.

Ravus's hand rested on the small of Val's back and she could feel the curl of nails against her spine. His voice was flat as he addressed Mabry. "Lady Silarial's mercy may be dreadful, but I have little choice but to throw myself on it. I know she came to talk to you—perhaps when she sees how unhappy you have been and how helpful you are, she will take you back to Court."

Mabry's mouth bent into a wry smile. "We all

must avail ourselves of her mercy. But now I want to do you a good turn for what you have done for me."

Val reached into her back pocket to give back Mabry's comb, the tines of it poking her fingers as she drew it out. Seaweed-wrapped pearls and tiny doves from the inside of sand dollars clung to the crest of the comb. Looking at it, Val suddenly saw the mermaid, necklace coiling in ropes of pearls and shell birds, dead eyes staring forever up at Val while her hair floated along the surface of the water, bereft of a matched comb.

Holding the comb in numb fingers, Val realized that it had come from a corpse.

"Mabry gave me this," Val said.

Ravus looked at it mildly, clearly not attaching any significance to it.

"It came from the mermaid," Val said. "She took this from the mermaid."

Mabry snorted. "Then, how is it that it came to be in your hand?"

"She gave it—"

Mabry turned to Ravus, interrupting Val smoothly. "Did you know she's been stealing from you—skimming off the top of your potions like a boggart drinks the head of cream off a bottle of milk?" Mabry snatched Val's arm, pushing up the sleeve so that Ravus could see the black marks

holly black

inside the crook of her elbow, the marks that looked like someone had put out a cigarette in her flesh. "And look what she's been doing—stuffing her veins with our balm. Now, Ravus, you tell me who's the poisoner. Will you suffer for her mistakes?"

Val reached her hand toward Ravus. He pulled back.

"What have you done?" he asked, tight-lipped.

"Yes, I shot up the potions," Val said. There was no point in denying anything now.

"Why would you do that?" he asked. "I thought it was harmless, just something to keep the Folk from pain."

"Never . . . it gives you . . . it makes humans . . . like faeries." That wasn't it, not exactly, but his face already said, *You didn't mind that I was monstrous because you are a monster.*

"I had thought better of you," Ravus said. "I had thought everything of you."

"I'm sorry," Val said. "Please, let me explain."

"*Humans*," he said, the word soaked with repugnance. "Liars, all of you. Now I understand my mother's hate."

"I might have lied about that but I'm not lying about the comb. I'm not lying about everything."

He grabbed Val's shoulder, his fingers so heavy she felt as if she was held by stone. "Now

I know what you saw in me to love. Potions."

"No!" Val said.

When she looked up at Ravus's face, there was nothing there that was familiar, nothing that was kind. His clawed thumb pressed against the pulse of her throat. "I think it is time that you were gone."

Val hesitated. "Just let me—"

"Go!" he shouted, pushing her away from him and curling his fingers into a fist so tight that his claws cut the pads of his own hand.

Val stumbled back, her throat stinging.

Ravus turned to Mabry. "Say that you feel revenged on me. At least tell me that."

"Not at all," Mabry replied with a sour smile. "I did you a good turn."

Val went, retracing her steps along the path, through the wall of fog, the woods and up to the castle, her eyes blurry and her heart aching. There, watching the distant flicker of the city lights, Val thought suddenly of her mother. Was this how she had felt, after Tom and Val were gone? Had she wanted to go back and change everything, but lacked the power?

Crawling along the rocks, Val saw the red tip of Ruth's clove cigarette before she saw the rest of their makeshift camp. Ruth stood up when Val got close. "I thought you left me again."

Val looked over at Lolli and Luis, curled up together. Luis looked different, his eyes circled darkly and his skin pale. "I just went for a walk."

Ruth took another long drag, the end of her cigarette sparking. "Yeah, well, your friend Dave just went for a walk, too."

Val thought about the revel and wondered if Dave had been there, another sweet tooth, wandering dazed among capricious masters.

"I . . . I," Val sat down, overwhelmed, and covered her face with her hands. "I fucked up. I really, really fucked up."

"What do you mean?" Ruth sat down next to Val and put her arm over her shoulder.

"It's too hard to explain. There are faeries, like real Final Fantasy faeries, and they've been poisoned and this stuff I've been taking—it's kind of a drug, but it's kind of magic, too." Val could feel tears trickle over her face, and swiped at them.

"You know," Ruth said, "people don't cry when they're sad. Everyone thinks that, but it's not true. People cry when they're frustrated or overwhelmed."

The mermaid's comb was still in Val's hand, she

realized, but she'd been clutching it so tightly that it had broken into pieces. Just thin sheets of shell, nothing more. No reason to think it proved anything.

"Look, I'll admit you sound a little crazy," Ruth said. "But so what? Even if you are completely delusional, we still have to work out your delusion, right? An imaginary problem needs an imaginary solution."

Val let her head fall onto Ruth's shoulder, relaxing in a way she hadn't relaxed since before she'd seen her mother and Tom and maybe before that. She'd forgotten how much she loved talking to Ruth.

"Okay, so start at the start."

"When I came to the city, I was just operating on autopilot," Val said. "I had tickets to the game, so I went. I know it sounds insane. Even when I was doing it, I thought it was crazy, like I was one of those people who kills their boss and then sits back down at their computer to finish reports.

"When I ran into Lolli and Dave, I just wanted to lose myself, to be nothing, to be nothingness. That sounds all wrong and dumb, I know."

"Very poetic." Ruth smirked. "Kind of goth."

Val rolled her eyes, but smiled. "They introduced me to some faeries and that's the part where everything stops making sense."

holly black

"Faeries? Like elves, goblins, trolls? Like the ones on Brian Froud panties at Hot Topic?"

"Look, I—"

Ruth held up her hand. "Just checking. Okay, faeries. I'm going with it."

"They have trouble with the iron, so there's this stuff that Lolli calls Nevermore. Never. It keeps them from getting too sick. Humans can . . . take it . . . and it makes you able to create illusions or to make people feel the way you want them to. We were doing deliveries of it for Ravus—he's the one that makes the Never—and we would take some for ourselves."

Ruth nodded. "Okay. So Ravus is a faerie?"

"Something like that," Val said. She could see a laugh in Ruth's eyes and was grateful when it didn't move to her lips. "Some of the Folk died of poison and they blamed Ravus. I think this comb came from one of the dead faeries and Mabry had it and I just don't know what that means.

"Everything is so crazy. Dave turned that cop into a dog on purpose and Mabry told Ravus we were stealing from him so he thinks I had something to do with the deaths and I haven't had Never in two days and my whole body hurts." It was true, the aches had started up again, the pain dim but growing, the temporary reprieve of faerie fruit not enough to keep her veins from clamoring for more.

Ruth squeezed Val's shoulders in a sideways hug. "Shit. Okay, that's crazy. What can we do?"

"We can figure it out," Val said. "I have all these clues; I just don't know how they fit together."

Val looked at the remains of the comb and thought of the mermaid again. Ravus had said rat poison killed the faerie, but rat poison was a dangerous and unlikely substance for a faerie poisoner to use, especially an alchemist like Ravus. And why would he want to kill a bunch of harmless faeries?

A human could have done it. A human courier was expected, not at all suspicious.

Val remembered the first delivery she'd ever been on and the bottle of Never Dave had unstoppered, breaking the wax. Shouldn't Mabry have been worried? With all the poisonings, wasn't that like taking an aspirin with the safety seal broken? The only way that anyone would do that was if they already knew who the poisoner was or if they were the poisoner themselves.

And Mabry had known that Val was using. Someone was telling her.

"But why?" Val said out loud.

"Why what?" asked Ruth.

holly black

Val stood up and paced on the rock. "I'm thinking. What's the result of the poisonings? Ravus gets in trouble!"

"So?" Ruth asked.

"So Mabry wants revenge on him," Val said. Of course: Revenge for the death of her lover. Revenge for her exile.

Mabry then. Mabry and a human accomplice. Dave was obvious, since he'd been the one that didn't bother to disguise that he was skimming Never from Mabry, but what reason did he have to kill faeries?

It could have been Luis. He hated faeries for what they'd done to his eye. He wore all that metal to protect himself. And he was using the Never, as the marks under his knee proved, even if he denied it. But for what if he couldn't see glamour? And why didn't he care that Dave had gone missing? Why pick now to hook up with Lolli when she'd wanted him for longer than Val had known her? He was so unworried. It was as though he knew where his brother was.

Val stopped at that thought.

"This is what we have to do," Val said. "We have to go to Mabry's house while she's still at the revel and find proof that she's behind the poisonings." Proof that would convince Ravus that she was innocent and proof that would convince the others he wasn't the poisoner at all. Proof that would save him so that he would forgive her.

"Okay," said Ruth, shouldering her backpack. "Let's go help your imaginary friends."

Chapter 11

*Strike a glass, and it will not endure an instant; simply
do not strike it, and it will endure a thousand years.*
—G. K. CHESTERTON, ORTHODOXY

Val and Ruth made it to Riverside Park in the cold
hours before dawn. The sky was deep dark and the
streets were hushed. Val's heart beat rabbit-fast,
adrenaline and muscle cramping keeping her from
noticing the chill air or the late hour. Ruth shivered and wrapped her monster-fur coat tighter as
the wind blew up off the water. Her cheeks were
streaked with makeup, smudged by tears and
careless hands, but when she smiled at Val, Ruth
looked like her old, confident self.

The park itself was mostly empty, with a small
group of people huddled near one of the walls,
one of them smoking what smelled like a joint. Val
looked down the row of apartment buildings
across from the park, but none of them was quite
right. She picked out the clogged fountain she'd
stood at days earlier, but when she looked across
the street, the door facing her was the wrong color

and there was a metal grate over the windows.

"Well?" Ruth asked.

Val shifted her weight. "I'm not sure."

"What are we going to do if you find it?"

Looking up, Val saw a gargoyle in a place slightly different from where she remembered, but the stone monster was enough to convince her that the house she was looking at had to be Mabry's. Perhaps her memory was just off.

"Watch for anyone coming," Val said, starting to cross the road. Her heart thundered in her chest. She had no idea what she was getting them into.

Ruth hurried after her. "Great. Lookout. I'm a lookout. Another thing to put on my college applications. What do I do if I see someone?"

Val looked back. "I'm not sure, actually."

Staring at the building for a long moment, Val grabbed hold of one of the gutter rings on the downspout and hoisted herself up the wall. It was like climbing a tree, like climbing a rope in gym class.

"What are you doing?" Ruth called, her voice shrill.

"What did you think I needed a lookout for? Now shut up."

Val climbed higher, her feet pushing against

holly black

the brick of the building, her fingers digging into the loops of metal as the gutter groaned and dented under her scrambling weight. As she reached for a windowsill, she found her hand in the mouth of a gargoyle, its chicken-bred-with-terrier face tilted to one side, eyes wide with surprise or excitement. She snatched her fingers back moments before the stone teeth snapped closed. Off balance, she kicked at the air for a moment, her full weight on the gutter and her one hand. The aluminum bent, tearing free of the supports.

Val jammed her foot into the brick and heaved hard, jumping and scrambling to catch the ledge. She heard a high-pitched squeak from below as she grabbed hold of the windowsill. Ruth. For a moment, she just hung on, afraid to move. Then she pulled herself up along the molding and pushed the window. It stuck, and for a moment she was afraid it was locked or painted shut, but she pushed harder and it gave. Climbing inside, past the tangled curtains, Val found herself in Mabry's bedroom. The floor was gleaming marble and the bed was a curving canopy of willow branches, piled with rumpled silks and satins. One side of the bed was clean, but the other was dusted with dirt and brambles.

Val went out into the hall. There was a series

of doors that opened into empty rooms and a staircase of ebonized wood. She walked down it and into the parlor, the squeak of the floorboards and the splash of the fountain the only sounds she heard.

The parlor was like she remembered, but the furniture seemed differently arranged and one of the doorways appeared larger. Val walked out of the apartment and into the main hallway, careful to brace Mabry's door open. She flipped the lock on the front door and jerked it open. Ruth gaped at her for a moment from the sidewalk, then ran inside.

"You've gone crazy," Ruth said. "We just broke into some posh building."

"It's protected by glamour," Val said. "It has to be." For the first time, Val considered the two doors she'd assumed went to other apartments. One was set opposite the door to Mabry's, the other at the end of the hall. Given the size of the rooms and the staircase in Mabry's apartment and the size of the building from the outside, it didn't seem possible that the doors led to anywhere at all. Val shook her head to clear it. It didn't matter. What mattered was that she found some evidence to implicate Mabry, something that would prove she had poisoned the other fey, prove it not just to

holly black

Ravus, but to Greyan and anyone else who thought Ravus was behind the deaths.

"At least it's warm in here," Ruth said, walking into the apartment and turning around on the gleaming marble floor. Her voice echoed in the nearly empty rooms. "If we have to be cat burglars, I'm going to see what's to steal in the fridge."

"We're trying to find evidence she's a poisoner. Just a thought before you start putting random things in your mouth." Ruth shrugged and walked past Val.

A display cabinet rested in one corner of the sitting room. Val peered through the glass. There was a bit of bark inside, braided with crimson hair; a figurine of a ballerina, her arms on her hips and her shoes red as roses; the broken neck of a bottle; and a faded and browned flower. Val thought she remembered different bizarre treasures from her earlier visit.

It made Val conscious of how impossible her task was. How would she know evidence, even if she saw it? Ravus might recognize these objects— know their uses and perhaps even part of their history, but she could make nothing of them.

It was hard to imagine Mabry as sentimental, but she must have been once, before Tamson's death made her hateful.

"Hey," Ruth said from the next room. "Look at this."

Val followed her voice. She was in the music room, beside the lap harp, sitting on an ottoman covered in an odd, pinkish leather. The body of the instrument looked to be gilded wood, carved with acanthus swirls, and each of the strings was a different shade. Most of them were brown or gold or black, but a few were red and one was leaf green.

Ruth knelt down beside it.

"Don't—," Val said, but Ruth's fingers brushed a brown string. Immediately a wailing flooded the room.

"Once I was a lady in waiting to the Queen Nicnevin," a voice full of tears intoned, accent rich and strange. "I was her favorite, her confidante, and I took my pleasure in harrying the others. Nicnevin had a particular toy, a Knight from the Seelie Court that she was overfond of. His tears of hate gave her more pleasure than another's cries of love. I was called before the Queen—she demanded to know if I was intriguing with him. I was not. Then she held up a pair of his gloves and demanded that I look at the embroidery along the cuffs. It was a careful pattern sewn with my own hair. There was more proof—sightings of us together, a note in his hand swearing devotion, none of it true. I fell down, begging Nicnevin, wild with fear. As they led me to my death, I saw one of the other ladies, Mabryn, smiling, her eyes bright as needles, her fingers reaching out to pluck a single strand of hair from my head. Now I must tell my tale forevermore."

"Nicnevin?" Ruth asked. "Who is that supposed to be?"

"I think she's the old Unseelie Queen," Val said. She dragged her fingers across several cords at once. A cacophony of voices rose up, each one telling its bitter tale, each one mentioning Mabry. "They're all hair. The hair of Mabry's victims."

"This is some spooky-ass shit," Ruth said.

"Shhh," Val said. One of the voices sounded familiar, but she couldn't quite place where she'd heard it before. She plucked a golden string.

"Once I was a courtier in the service of the Queen Silarial," a male voice said. "I lived for sport, for riddles, and dueling and dance. Then I fell in love and all those things ceased to matter. My only joy was in Mabry. I desired a thing only if it delighted her. I basked in her gladness. Then, one lazy afternoon, as we gathered flowers to weave into garlands, I saw that she'd wandered off. I followed and overheard her speaking with a creature from the Unseelie Court. They seemed well acquainted and her voice was soft as she told him the information she had gathered for the Unseelie Queen. I should have been angry, but I was too afraid for her. If Silarial had found out, the consequences would have been terrible. I told Mabry that I would tell no one, but that she must leave directly. She told me she would and wept bitterly over deceiving me. Two days later I was to duel in a tournament with a friend. When I donned my armor, it felt strange, lighter, but I paid it no mind. Mabry told me she'd stitched her own hair into it as a token. When my friend struck, the armor crumbled and the sword cut me right through. I felt the silk of her hair against my face and knew I was betrayed. Now I must tell my tale forevermore."

Val sat down hard, staring at the harp. Mabry was a spy for the Unseelie Court. She had killed Tamson herself. Ravus had only been her instrument.

"Who was that?" Ruth asked. "Did you know him?"

Val shook her head. "Ravus did, though. He was the one swinging the sword in that story."

Ruth bit her lower lip. "This is so complicated. How are we going to figure out anything?"

"We already figured out something," Val said.

She stood up and walked into the next room.

holly black

It was the kitchen. There was no stove, however; no refrigerator, only a sink in a long expanse of polished slate. Val opened up one of the cabinets, but it was filled only with empty jars.

Val thought about Ravus's glamoured form, his golden eyes the flaw in his disguise. There was something disquieting about these perfect rooms, dustless and without even a stray hair or bit of grime, echoing only with footsteps and the splash of water. But if there was a glamour, she had no idea what was beneath it.

Ruth walked into the room and Val noticed the white powder drizzling from her backpack.

"What's that?" Val asked.

"What?" Ruth looked behind her, on the floor, and shouldered off the bag. She laughed. "Looks like I ripped the canvas and popped a hole in our baby."

"Shit. This is worse than a bread-crumb trail. Mabry's going to know we were in here."

Ruth squatted down and started sweeping the powder together with her hands. Instead of forming a pile, it gusted up in white clouds.

As Val looked at the flour, she got an idea. "Wait. Hey, I think I might have to commit infanticide."

Ruth shrugged and pulled out the sack. "I

guess we can always have another one."

Val ripped open the paper packaging and started sprinkling flour on the floor. "There has to be something here, something we can't see."

Ruth grabbed a handful of white powder and threw it at the door. Val tossed another fistful. Soon the air was thick with it. Their hair was covered and when they breathed, flour coated their tongues.

It settled all over the apartment, showing the fish pond as a broken pipe spilling water into buckets and pooling on the floor, revealing the sagging sheetrock of the ceiling, the chipped tiles along the walls and tracks of mouse droppings on the floor.

"Look." Ruth walked over to one of the walls, powder making her ghostly. Flour was stuck to most of the wall, but there was a large bare patch.

Val tossed more powder at the gap, but instead of hitting the wall, it seemed to go through the space.

"We got it." Val grinned and lifted her fist. "Wonder twin powers activate!"

Ruth grinned back, knocking her fist into Val's. "Shape of two fucking lunatics."

"Speak for yourself," Val said, and ducked through the gap.

There, in a shadowed room hung with velvet

drapes, was Luis. He lay on a carpet patterned with pomegranates and was wrapped in a woolen blanket, but despite that, he was shivering. There was blood on his scalp and several of his braids had been cut off.

At first Val just gaped at him. "Luis?" she finally managed.

He looked up, squinting, as though against a bright light. "Val?" He scrambled to a sitting position. "Where's Dave? Is he all right?"

"I don't know," she said absently. Her mind was racing. "What are you doing here?"

"Can't you see that I'm chained to the floor?" Luis said. He turned his wrists and she saw that his own braids were wrapped around them, pulled taut.

"The floor?" Val repeated stupidly. "But what about the carpet?"

Luis laughed. "I suppose this place looks beautiful to you."

Val looked at the low couches, the bookshelves overflowing with cloth-covered fairy stories, the faded grandeur of the carpet and painted molding on the walls. "It's one of the most gorgeous rooms I've ever been in."

"The plaster walls are cracked and there's a leak in the ceiling that pretty much means that whole corner is black with mold. There's no furniture here, either, and certainly no rug—just floorboards with some old nails sticking up out of them."

Val looked around at the soft light coming from a pewter lamp with a fringed shade. "Then what is it that I'm seeing?"

"Glamour, what else?"

Ruth ducked her head into the room. "What's goi— Luis?"

"Hold on. How can we be sure it's really you, Luis?" Val asked.

"Who else would I be?"

Ruth came most of the way in, her foot still in the glamoured opening, as though she thought it might close at any moment without a wedge. "We just left you in the park and you were sleeping."

Luis let his head fall back. "Yeah, well, the last time I saw Ruth, I was with Lolli and Dave in the park. We'd picked out a place to sleep near the weather castle. Lolli was leaned up against me, dozing off when Dave just got up and walked off. I knew he was upset. Shit, I was freaking out, too. I thought maybe he wanted to be alone.

"But then he didn't come back and I didn't know what to think. I went out looking. I saw him walking back through the Ramble. He wasn't

holly black

alone, either. At first I thought it was some guy—I don't know, hitting on him—but then I saw the guy had feathers instead of hair. I started toward them and that's when tiny fingers covered my mouth and my good eye, grabbed hold of my arms and my legs. I could hear them snickering as they lifted me up into the air and my brother saying, 'Don't worry. It's just for a little while.' I didn't know what to think. I sure didn't think I'd wind up here."

"Did you see Mabry?" Val asked. "Did she say anything to you?"

"Not much. She was distracted by something that was going down. Someone visited her and she was pissed about it."

"There's something we have to tell you," Val said.

Luis went quiet, his mouth pressed into a thin line. "What?" he asked, and his voice was so quiet that it made Val's heart ache.

"It was Dave that we thought was missing. He's gone. Someone's pretending to be you."

"So you came here looking for Dave?"

"We came here looking for evidence. I think Mabry's behind all the faerie deaths."

Luis scowled. "Wait, so where's my brother? Is he in trouble?"

Val shook her head. "I don't think so. Whatever's pretending to be you seems to be spending all its time screwing Lolli. I don't think that's exactly on the supernatural agenda, but it's definitely on Dave's."

Luis winced, but he said nothing.

"We should hurry," Ruth said, patting Val's head, her fingers threading through the stubble. "Just because this bitch can't tie you up with your own hair doesn't mean we should hang around."

"Right." Val leaned over Luis, looking at the braids that bound him to the floor. She tried to snap them or pull them loose, but they were as hard as if they were made of steel.

"Mabry cut them with scissors," Luis said. "She fucking scalped me, too."

"Do you think scissors would cut the braids?" Ruth asked.

Val nodded. "She has to have a way to cut through her own spells. Where do you think they would be?"

"I don't know," Luis said. "They might not even look like scissors."

Val stood up and walked out into the parlor, stopping at the fountain where the flour had dissolved, then walked over to the display cabinet.

"Do you see anything?" Val called.

holly black

Ruth pulled out a drawer and dumped the contents onto the floor. "Nothing."

Val looked in the cabinet, noticing the ballerina again, noticing the loops her arms made and the bloody color of the toe shoes. Reaching in, Val picked her up, sticking her fingers through the arm gaps and pushing. The figurine's legs closed and opened, just like scissors.

"Get the harp," Val said. "I'll get Luis."

It wasn't quite dawn when they picked their way back through the Ramble, up through the branching trails to where they'd left Lolli and what had appeared to be Luis. The strings of the harp jangled as they moved, but Ruth muffled it by hugging it tighter to her chest. As Val, Ruth, and Luis approached, they saw that the other Luis was awake.

Lolli's voice was high and trembling. "It's so cold and you're burning up with fever."

The disguised Luis looked at them. His eyes were blackened around the edges and his mouth was dark. His skin was pale as paper and had a sheen of sweat over it that made it appear like plastic. With trembling fingers, he brought a cigarette to his lips. The smoke didn't leave his body.

"Dave," the real Luis said. His voice was even, calm, just like Val's had been after she'd seen her mother with Tom. It was a voice so full of emotion that it sounded like no emotion at all.

Lolli looked at Luis, and then at his twin. "Wha—what's happening?"

"You couldn't tell the difference, could you?" the disguised Luis said to Lolli. His face changed, features subtly shifting to become Dave's. The blackened mouth and eyes remained, as did the sheen on his skin.

Lolli gasped.

He laughed like a maniac, his voice raspy. "You couldn't even tell the difference, but you would never give me a chance."

"You fucking shit." Lolli slapped Dave. She hit him again, blows raining against the hands he threw up to ward her off.

Luis grabbed her arms, but Dave laughed again. "You think you know me? I'm Sketchy Dave? Dave the Coward? Dave the Idiot? Dave who needs his brother's protection? I don't need nothing." He looked Luis in the face. "You're so smart, right? So smart you didn't see any of this coming. Who's the moron, huh? You got some fancy fucking word for how stupid you are?"

"What have you done?" Luis asked.

"He made a deal with Mabry," Val said. "Didn't you?"

holly black

Dave smiled, but it looked like a rictus grin, the skin of his mouth too tight. When he spoke, Val saw only blackness beyond his teeth, as though she were looking into a dark tunnel. "Yeah, I did a deal. I don't need the Sight to know when I have something somebody wants." He wiped his forehead, eyes increasingly wide. "I wanted—"

He collapsed, his body shaking. Luis sank to his knees next to Dave and reached out to smooth his dreads back from his face, then abruptly pulled his hand back. "He's way too hot. It's like his skin is on fire."

"Never," Val said. "He's been using Never much more than once a day. He had to take it this whole time to keep that shape."

"In the movies they put people with crazy fevers in a bathtub with ice," Ruth said.

"What, when they O.D. on faerie drugs?" Lolli snapped.

"Grab him," Val said. "The lake should be cold enough."

Luis slid his hands under his brother's shoulders. "Be careful. His body is really warm."

"Take my gloves." Ruth pulled a pair out of her coat pocket and handed them to Val.

Pulling them on quickly, she grabbed Dave's ankles. Touching his skin was like grabbing the handle of a pot of boiling water. She lifted. He was so light, he might have been hollow.

Together she and Luis hurried down the steps, down the paths of the Ramble to the edge of the water. The heat of Dave's body scorched her skin through the gloves and he twitched and writhed as if he were fighting some unseen force. Val gritted her teeth and held on.

Luis waded into the water and Val followed, the frigid cold at her calves a terrible contrast to the burn of her hands.

"Okay, down," Luis said.

They lowered Dave into the water, his body steaming as it touched the lake. Val let go and started back to the shore, but Luis held on, keeping his brother's head above water, like a preacher performing a terrible baptism.

"Is it helping?" Ruth called.

Luis nodded, rubbing his brother's floating face. Val could see that Luis's hand was bright pink, but whether he was burned or just cold she wasn't sure. "Better, but we have to get him to a hospital."

Lolli waded in, staring down at Dave. "You fucking moron," she shouted. "How could you be so stupid?" She looked suddenly lost. "Why would he do this for me?"

holly black

"You can't feel responsible," Val said. "If I were you, I think I'd want to kill him."

"I don't know what to feel," Lolli said.

"Val," said Luis. "We have to go ask Ravus for help."

"Ravus?" Ruth demanded.

"He saved his life before," Luis said.

Val thought of Ravus's face, closed, his eyes dark with fury. She thought of the things she knew about Mabry and the things she just guessed about the currency Dave had used to pay for her help. "I don't know if he'll be willing to now."

"I'll take Dave to the hospital," Lolli said.

"Go with her, okay?" Val asked Ruth. "Please."

"Me?" Ruth looked disbelieving. "I don't even know him."

Val leaned close to her. "But I know you."

Ruth rolled her eyes. "Fine. But you owe me. You owe me like a month of mute servitude."

"I owe you like a year of mute servitude," Val said and waded into the water to help Luis lift his brother's body once more. Slowly they made their way to the street. The first cab they hailed pulled up and then, seeing Dave's body, drove off before Lolli could grab hold of the door. The next one stopped, seemingly indifferent as the two girls got in and Luis draped his writhing brother across their laps.

"Here," Ruth said, handing over the harp.

"We'll take care of him," Lolli said.

"I'll be there as soon as I can." Luis hesitated shutting the door.

The taxi started to move and Val saw Ruth's pale face staring from the back window, her lips mouthing something Val couldn't make out as the car got farther and farther away.

Chapter 12

And her sweet red lips on these lips of mine
Burned like the ruby fire set
In the swinging lamp of a crimson shrine,
Or the bleeding wounds of the pomegranate,
Or the heart of the lotus drenched and wet
With the spilt-out blood of the rose-red wine.

—OSCAR WILDE, "IN THE GOLD ROOM: A HARMONY"

A horse-drawn carriage had stopped beneath the arch of the bridge support. It was a long way from the park or anywhere else that a carriage should be and the dun horse looked restless in the pale, dawn light. There was no driver.

"Do you think someone took a ride to the supermarket?" Val asked.

"That's no horse," Luis said, pulling Val wide of it. His eyes were bloodshot, his lips cracked with cold. "Be glad you can't see what it really is."

It looked like any other city horse, with its big sagging back and fat hooves. Val squinted at it until the image blurred, but she still didn't know what Luis saw and she decided not to ask. "Come on."

Sticking near the opposite wall, she crept beneath the overpass, Luis right behind her. She knocked on the stump, but as they slipped through the doorway, Val heard someone banging down the bridge stairs.

It was too late for them to do anything but gape at Greyan. His hands were covered in blood, blood that dripped off the tips of his fingers and clotted on the dusty steps, too bright to seem real. He held his bronze knives together in one hand. They, too, glistened with gore.

"It is done," the ogre said. He looked tired. "Little humans, let me lesson you to intrude no more in the dealings of the fey."

"Where's Ravus?" Val demanded. "What happened?"

"Would you fight me again, mortal? Your loyalty is commendable, if misplaced. Save your courage for a more worthy foe." He pushed past her and walked down the remaining steps. "I have no lust for dealing more death today."

Everything narrowed to that moment, that word. Death. *Surely not,* Val told herself, touching the cold stone wall for support. For a moment, she didn't think she could walk the rest of the way up the stairs. She couldn't bear it.

Luis walked slowly up the steps, up to the

holly black

landing, and then back down. He brought his finger to his lips. "She's in there."

Val started moving, too fast, and Luis's hand clamped down on her arm. "Quiet," he hissed.

Val nodded, not daring to ask about Ravus. Together, they inched up the steps, each footfall causing a little puff of dust, the creak of the iron frame, the jangle of the harp strings, things that Val hoped were hidden by the steady rumble of traffic overhead. As they neared the landing, she heard Mabry's voice, full of anxiety. "Where do you keep it? I know you have to have some poison somewhere. Come now, do me one last service."

Val waited to hear Ravus's answer, but he didn't speak.

Luis looked grim.

"You used to be so eager to please," Mabry went on bitterly. Something fell inside the room and Val thought she heard the sharp sound of shattering glass.

Val crept forward, parting the plastic sheeting. Ravus's desk was turned over, his books and papers scattered across the room. The armchair was sliced cleanly across the back, leaking feathers and foam. A few candles flickered from the floor, some encircled with rivulets of wax. The stone of the walls was grooved with deep cuts. Ravus lay stretched out on his back, one hand over his chest as blood rose between his fingers. Dark, wet streaks painted the floor, as though he had crawled across it. Mabry bent over a cabinet, one hand rummaging through the contents, the other holding a dish that contained the red remains of something.

Val crawled closer, heedless of Luis's warning fingers digging into her skin, fear numbing her to anything but the sight of Ravus's body.

"Do you know how long I've waited for you to die?" Mabry asked, her voice almost frantic now. "Finally, I would be free from exile. Free to return to the Bright Court and my work. But now all the pleasure I thought to have from your death is robbed from me.

"Someone has to appear to have murdered all those faeries, so at least you were good for one thing. No one likes loose ends." Mabry selected a vial from the cabinet and took a breath. "This will have to do—my new Lady is impatient and wants things taken care of before Midwinter. Isn't it ironic that after all this time, after all your loyalty, it is I who was chosen to be her agent in the Unseelie Court? I would not have thought the Queen of the Seelie Court would want a double agent of her own. Perhaps I can come to enjoy working for

Silarial. After all, she's proven to be as ruthless a mistress as my own dear Lady."

Val parted the plastic sheeting and crawled into the room. Ravus's head was turned toward the wall where Tamson's sword hung, his golden eyes dull and unfocused. There was a deep pit in his chest that his hand half-covered, as though he were pledging something in death. The room reeked of a weird, heavy sweetness that made Val want to gag.

I cross my heart and hope to die.

Val was shaking as she stood, no longer caring about Mabry, about politics or plans or anything except Ravus.

She couldn't look away from the blood that stained the edges of his lips and pinked his teeth. His skin was far too pale, the green of it the only color left.

Mabry spun, the plate in her hand clearly holding the piece of flesh missing from Ravus's chest. His heart. Val felt dizziness threaten to overwhelm her. She wanted to scream, but her throat closed up on the sound.

"Luis," said Mabry, "your brother will be sorry to hear you tired so quickly of my hospitality."

Val half-turned. Luis was standing behind her, a muscle in his jaw trembling.

"And my harp." Mabry's voice held a certain, teasing pleasure that was at odds with their surroundings, with the broken furnishings and the blood. "Ravus, look what your servants have brought. A little music."

"Why are you talking to him?" Val shouted. "Can't you see he's dead?"

At the sound of her voice, Ravus shifted his head slightly. "Val?" he groaned.

Val jumped, edging back, away from his body. It wasn't possible for him to speak. Hope warred with horror and she felt the gorge rise in her throat.

"Go ahead, Luis," Mabry said. "Play it. I'm sure he would rest easier knowing."

Luis strummed one string and Tamson's voice echoed through the chamber, recounting his tale. In the moment that Tamson said the word "betrayed," the glass sword fell from the wall, cracking deep under the surface, like ice on a lake.

"Tamson," Ravus said softly. His head came up, eyes hard with hate, but his arm was too slippery with blood to support him. He fell back with a groan.

Mabry's lip curled and she stalked over to Ravus. "Oh, to see your face when you stuck your sword through him. Your hair will be the next

holly black

string in my harp, wailing your pathetic story for all time."

"Get away from him," Val said, picking up the broken leg of a table.

Mabry held up the plate. "Surprising, isn't it, that trolls can live a time without their hearts? He's got perhaps an hour if I don't hurry him along, but I'll dash his heart to the ground if you don't stay out of my way."

Val went still, dropping the wood.

"Well and good," Mabry said. "I'll leave him in your capable hands."

Her hooves clattered down the steps, gown sweeping after her.

Val dropped to her knees beside Ravus. A long, clawed finger reached up to touch her face. His lips were smeared a dark crimson. "I wished for you to come. I shouldn't have, but I did."

"Tell me what to bring you," Val said. "What herbs to combine."

He shook his head. "This I cannot heal."

"Then I'll go get your heart." Val said, her voice hard. She jumped up, ducking through the plastic and down the stairs. She hit the wall and pushed through the doorway onto the street. The cold air stung her hot face, but both Mabry and the carriage were gone.

Everything had spun madly, dizzily, so far out of control that she couldn't stop it. There was no way. No plan.

The only thing she had any power over was herself. She could walk away from here, run away again and again until she was so cold and numb that she felt nothing at all. At least she would be the one making the decision; she would be *in control.* She wouldn't have to watch Ravus die.

There, squatting on the sidewalk, she choked with dry-eyed sobs. It was like being sick when there was nothing left in her stomach. She ground her nails into the wrist of her hand, the pain focusing her mind until she could force herself to walk back up the stairs and not scream.

Luis was kneeling near Ravus, their hands clasped.

"A cord of amaranth," the troll said hoarsely, a red bubble forming at his lip. "The sleep of a child, the scent of summer. Weave it into a crown for your brother and set it on his head with your own hands."

"I don't know how to get those things," Luis said, his voice breaking.

Val stared at them both, then at the wall and the dusty blinds. "Forgive me," she said.

Ravus turned to her, but she couldn't wait for his answer. She tugged at the cloth, ripping down

holly black

the curtains, and the room flooded with light. Dust motes danced through the air.

"What are you doing?" Luis screamed.

Val ignored him, rushing to the next window.

Ravus pushed himself up on one elbow. He opened his mouth to speak, but his skin had already gone to gray and his mouth froze, slightly parted, words silenced. He became stone, a statue made by the hand of some twisted sculptor, and the smeared blood turned to rubble.

Luis ran to where she was ripping down more drapes. "Are you crazy?"

"We need time to stop Mabry," Val shouted back. "He won't die while he's stone. He won't die until dusk."

Luis nodded slowly. "I thought I could—I didn't think of the sunlight."

"Ravus can weave the crown for Dave himself when he wakes up. That was what you asked him about, wasn't it?" Val picked up Tamson's sword, shining so brightly in the sunlight that she could not look at it directly. She held the hilt between the palms of her two hands. "We'll find Mabry and then we'll save them both."

Luis took a step back from her. "I thought magic swords weren't supposed to break."

Val sat down cross-legged on the floor, letting

the sword rest across her knees. The crack was visible underneath the glass, but when she ran her fingers over the surface, it was smooth.

"Mabry said something about being an agent in the Unseelie Court."

"A double agent." Luis spun the ball on his lip ring with his thumb and index finger as he considered. "And she was looking for poison."

"The faeries in the park said Silarial had come to see Mabry. They thought Mabry had some evidence. Maybe they made some kind of deal?"

"A deal for her to poison someone?"

"Okay," Val said. "If Silarial knew Mabry had been responsible for the poisoning of the Seelie exiles, then she really had Mabry over a barrel. She'd have to do whatever Silarial said to save her skin. Even go back to her own court and kill someone."

"My brother poisoned them, didn't he?" Luis asked.

"What?"

"That's what Dave did for Mabry. He poisoned all those faeries so it would look like Ravus was behind their deaths. What she did for Dave was tie me up in her house. That's what you meant when you said Silarial is responsible. You mean she orchestrated it, but someone else did the poisoning."

"I didn't mean that. We don't know that."

Luis said nothing.

"I'm surprised you care," Val said, frustration and fear making her snap. "I didn't think you would think killing faeries was all that big of a deal."

"You thought I was the killer, didn't you?" Luis turned his face away from her.

"Of course I did." Val knew she was being cruel, but the words poured past her lips like they were living things, like they were spiders and worms and beetles eager to get out of her mouth. "All your talk about faeries being dangerous and then, oh look, they're getting killed with rat poison. If you'd ever guessed Dave was the poisoner, what would you have done? Would you have really stopped him?"

"Of course I would have," Luis spat.

"Oh, come on. You hate faeries."

"I'm afraid of them," Luis shouted, then took a deep breath. "My dad had the Sight and it made him crazy. My mom's dead. My brother is catatonic. I'm a one-eyed fucking bum at seventeen. Faerieland must be a nonstop party."

"Well, then, break out the champagne," Val said, walking so close to him that she could feel the heat of his body. She swept her hand around the room. "Another one of them's dead."

"That's not what I meant." Luis turned away

from her, the light washing the color from his face. He walked to Ravus's body, reached out a hand to touch the stone, and then pulled back as though he was about to be burned. "I just don't know what we can do."

"Who do you think Silarial wants Mabry to poison? It has to be someone in the Unseelie Court."

"That's what Ravus called the Night Court."

Val walked to the map on the wall of Ravus's room. There, outside New York City, far from the pins marking each of the poisonings, were two black marks, one in Upstate New York, the other in New Jersey. She touched the one in Jersey. "Here."

"But who? This is way over our heads."

"Isn't there a new king there?" Val asked. "Mabry said something about Midwinter. Could he be the one she's supposed to make dead?"

"Maybe."

"Even if he isn't—it doesn't matter. All we need to know is where she is."

"But the Courts aren't places humans are supposed to be, especially the Unseelie Court. Most faeries won't even go there."

"We have to go—we have to get Ravus's heart. He's going to die if we don't."

holly black

"What are we going to do? Go down there and ask for it?"

"Pretty much," Val said. As she got up, she saw a tiny vial of Never lying beside asphodel and rose hips. She lifted it up.

"What's that for?" Luis asked, although he must have known perfectly well.

Her thoughts strayed to Dave, but even his pallid skin and blackened mouth didn't make her any less hungry for Never. She might need it. She needed it now. One pinch and all this pain would be gone.

But she stuffed it into her pack and fished out the return train tickets she'd bought weeks before, holding them out to Luis. The paper was so worn from riding around in her bag that it felt as soft as cloth between her fingers, but when Luis took his, the ticket sliced shallowly over her flesh. For a moment, her skin seemed so surprised that it forgot to bleed.

Chapter 13

Immediately after the monsters, die the heroes.

—ROBERTO CALASSO,

THE MARRIAGE OF CADMUS AND HARMONY

Val perched in her seat for a few moments, then paced restlessly in the aisle. Each time the conductor passed her, she asked him what the next stop was, were they running late, could they go faster. He said they couldn't. Glancing over at the sword swaddled in a dirty blanket and tied with shoelaces, he hurried on.

Val had had to show the hilt to prove that it was merely decorative when she boarded. It was only glass, after all. She'd explained that she was making a delivery.

Luis spoke softly into Val's cell, his head turned against the window. He'd called all the hospitals he could think of before he thought to call Ruth's

holly black

phone and now that he'd gotten her, his body had relaxed, his fingers no longer digging into the canvas of Val's backpack, jaw no longer clenched so tight that the muscles in his face jumped.

He clicked off the phone. "You only have a little power left."

Val nodded. "What did she say?"

"Dave is in critical condition. Lolli fucked off. She couldn't handle the hospital, hates the smell or something. They're giving Ruth a hard time because she won't tell them what Dave took, and, of course, they won't let her in to see him, 'cause she's not family."

Val fingered the torn edge of the plastic seat, nostrils flaring as she breathed hard. It was more fury, heaped on what already felt like too much fury to bear. "Maybe you—"

"Nothing I could do." Luis looked out the window. "He's not going to make it, is he?"

"He will," Val said firmly. She could save Ravus. Ravus could save Dave. Like black dominoes, set up in winding rows, and the most important thing was that she didn't tip over.

Looking at her own hands, splintered and smudged with dirt, it was hard to imagine that they would be the hands that saved anyone.

Her thoughts settled on the Never in her bag.

It promised to sing down her veins, to make her swifter and stronger and finer than she was. She wouldn't be stupid about it. She wouldn't wind up like Dave. Not more than a pinch. Not more than once today. She just needed it now, to keep herself together, to face Mabry, to let all the rage and sorrow be swallowed up into something larger than herself.

Luis settled on the other side of the seat, lying down as much as he could, eyes closed, arms folded across his chest, head pillowed on her backpack and pushed up against the metal lip of the window. He wouldn't know if she slipped into the bathroom.

Val stood, but something caught her eye. The cloth wrapping had slipped, revealing a little of the glass sword, ethereal in the sunlight. It made her think of icicles hanging from Ravus's mother's hair.

Balance. Like a well-made sword. Perfect balance.

She couldn't trust herself with Never working inside of her, making her alternately formidable or distracted, dreamy or intense. Off balance. Unbalanced. She didn't know how long she could keep herself from taking it, but she could keep putting it off for another moment. And maybe a

holly black

moment after that. Val bit her lip and resumed her pacing.

Val and Luis got off at the Long Branch station, pushing onto the concrete platform as soon as the doors opened. A few taxis idled nearby, roofs crowned by yellow caps.

"What do we do now?" Luis asked. "Where the hell are we?"

"We're going to my house," Val said. Holding the sword by its hilt, she leaned the wrapped blade against her shoulder and started walking. "We need to borrow a car."

The brick house looked smaller than Val remembered it. The grass was brown and leaf-covered, the trees black and bare. Val's mother's red Miata sat in front, parked on the street even though she should have been at work. Balled-up tissues and empty coffee cups littered the dashboard. Val frowned. It wasn't like her mother to be messy.

Val pulled open the screen door, feeling as if she were walking through a dream landscape. Everything was at once familiar and strange. The front door was unlocked, the television off in the living room. Despite the fact that it was past noon, the house was dark.

It was unnerving to be in the same place where

she had seen Tom draped over her mother, but weirder still was how small the room seemed. Somehow it had grown in her mind until it was so vast that she couldn't imagine crossing it to get back to her own bedroom.

Val swung the sword off her shoulder and dropped her backpack onto the couch. "Mom?" she called softly. There was no answer.

"Just find the keys," Luis said. "It's easier to get forgiveness than permission."

Val half-turned her head to snap at him, but movement on the stairs stopped her.

"Val," her mother said, rushing down the steps, only to stop at the lower landing. Her eyes were red-rimmed, her face un–made up, and her hair wild. Val felt everything at once: guilt at making her mother so upset, serves-her-right satisfaction that her mother was suffering, and profound exhaustion. She wanted them both to stop feeling so miserable, but she had no idea how to make that happen.

Val's mother walked the last few steps slowly and hugged her hard. Val leaned against her mother's shoulder, smelling soap and faint perfume. Eyes burning with sudden emotion, she pulled away.

"I was so worried. I kept thinking you would

holly black

come in, just like this, but you didn't. For days and days you didn't." Her mother's voice shrilled and broke.

"I'm here now," Val said.

"Oh, honey." Val's mother reached out hesitantly to stroke her fingers across Val's head. "You're so thin. And your hair—"

Val twisted out from under her hand. "Leave it, Mom. I like my hair."

Her mother blanched. "That's not what I meant. You always look beautiful, Valerie. You just look so different."

"I am different," Val said.

"Val," Luis warned. "The keys."

She scowled at him, took a breath. "I need to borrow the car."

"You've been gone for weeks." Val's mother looked at Luis for the first time. "You can't be leaving again."

"I'll be back tomorrow."

"No." Val's mother's voice had a note of panic in it. "Valerie, I'm so sorry. I'm sorry about everything. You don't know how worried I've been about you, the things that I've been imagining. I kept waiting for the phone call that would say the police had found you dead in a ditch. You can't put me through that again."

"There's something I have to do," Val said. "And I don't have much time. Look, I don't understand about you and Tom. I don't know what you were thinking or how it happened, but—"

"You must think that I—"

"But *I don't care anymore.*"

"Then why—," Val's mother started.

"This isn't about you and I can't come home until it's finished. Please."

Her mother sighed. "You failed your driving test."

"Can you drive?" Luis asked.

"I have my permit," Val said to her mother, then glanced at Luis. "I can drive fine. I just can't parallel park."

Val's mother padded into the kitchen and came back with a key and an alarm hanging from a keychain with a rhinestone "R" on it. "I owe you some trust, Valerie, so here it is. Don't make me regret it."

"I won't," Val said.

Val's mother dropped the keys into Val's hand. "You promise you'll be back tomorrow? Promise me."

Val thought of the way her lips had burned when she hadn't kept her promise to return to Ravus on time. She nodded. Luis opened the front door. Val turned toward it, not looking at her

holly black

mother. "You're still my mom," Val said.

As Val walked down her front steps, she felt the sun on her face, and it seemed that at least one thing might be okay.

Val drove the car through the familiar roads, reminding herself to signal and watch her speed. She hoped that no one would pull them over.

"You know," Luis said, "the last time I was in a car it was my grandma's Bug and we were going to the store for something on a holiday—Thanksgiving, I think. She lived out on Long Island where you need cars to get around. I remember it because my dad had pulled me aside earlier to tell me that he could see goblins in the garden."

Val said nothing. She was concentrating on the road.

She steered the Miata past the pillars that flanked the entrance of the graveyard, the brick of them covered by looping tendrils of leafless vines. The cemetery itself swelled into a hill, dotted with white stones and burial vaults. Despite the fact that it was late November, the grass there was still green.

"Do you see anything?" Val asked. "It just looks like any other cemetery to me."

Luis didn't answer at first. He stared out the window, one hand unconsciously coming up to touch the clouding glass. "That's because you're blind."

Val stepped on the brake, stopping them short. "What do you see?"

"They're everywhere." Luis put his hand on the door handle, his voice little more than breath.

"Luis?" Val turned off the car.

His voice sounded distant, as if he were speaking to himself. "God, look at them. Leathery wings. Black eyes. Long, clawed fingers." Then he looked over at Val, like he'd suddenly remembered her. "Get down!"

She lunged over, throwing her head into his lap, feeling the warmth of his arms coming down on her as air whipped over the top of the car.

"What's happening?" Val shouted over the keening of the wind. Something scratched at the leather roof of the car and the hood shook.

Then the air stilled, dropping away to nothing. As Val slowly lifted her head, it seemed to her that not even a leaf moved with a breeze. The whole graveyard had gone quiet.

"This whole car is fiberglass." Luis looked up. "They could claw right through the roof if they wanted to."

holly black

"Why don't they?"

"I'm guessing they're waiting to see if we're here to dump some flowers on a grave."

"They don't need to do that. We're coming out." Leaning into the backseat, Val unwrapped the glass sword. Luis grabbed Val's backpack and slung it over his shoulder.

Val closed her eyes and took a deep breath. Her stomach churned, the way it did before a lacrosse game, but this was different. Her body felt distant, mechanical. Her senses narrowed to notice every sound, each shift in color and shape, but little else. Adrenaline called to her blood, chilling her fingers, speeding her heart.

Looking down at the sword, Val opened the door and stepped out onto the gravel. "I come in peace," she said. "Take me to your leader."

Invisible fingers closed on her skin, pinching the flesh, tearing at her hair, pushing and pulling her into the hill, where clumps of grass rose up and scampered away from the black dirt. She tried to scream as she fell forward, facedown in the earth, breathing the rich mineral smell as she choked on her shriek. Her arms pushed against the soil as she tried to lever herself up, but the dirt and rock and grass gave beneath her and she tumbled down into the root-wrapped darkness.

• • •

Val awoke in golden chains in a hall filled with faeries.

On a dais of dirt, a white-haired knight sat on a throne of braided birch, its bark as pale as bone. He leaned forward and beckoned to a green-skinned, winged girl who regarded Val with black, alien eyes. The winged faerie leaned down and spoke softly to the knight on the throne. His lips twisted into what might have been a smile.

Above her was the underside of the hill, hollow as a bowl, and hung with long roots that grasped and turned as though they were fingers that couldn't quite reach what they desired.

All around Val a bevy of creatures whispered and winked and wondered at her. Some were tall and thin as sticks, others tiny creatures that flitted through the air like Needlenix had. Some had horns that twisted back from their brows like vines, some tossed back mottled green manes as thick as thread on a spool, and a few tripped along on strange and unlikely feet. Val flinched back from one girl with powdery wings and fingers that deepened in color from moonstone white to blue at the tips. There was no place she could look and see anything familiar. She was all the way down the rabbit hole now, right at the very bottom.

holly black

A shrunken man with long golden hair went down on one knee in front of the creature on the throne and then rose as nimbly as if he were a boy. He looked slyly in Val's direction. "They found the entrance as easily as if they were directed, but who would direct a pair of humans? A conundrum for your pleasure and delight, my Lord Roiben."

"As you say." Roiben nodded to him and the faerie man stepped back.

"I can address this mystery," a familiar voice said.

Val rolled onto her back, banging up against Luis's body, and twisting her head toward the speaker. Luis grunted. Mabry stepped over them, the hem of her ruddy gown brushing Val's cheek. She held out a sculpted silver box and sank into a shallow curtsy. "I have what they seek."

Roiben raised a single white brow. "My Court is not pleased to have sunlight make merry and dance in our halls, even if it is only for a moment's admission of prisoners."

Luis rolled on his side and Val could see that he was chained like she was, but that his face was bloody. Each of his steel piercings had been cut from his flesh.

Mabry cast her eyes down, but she didn't look very abashed. "Allow me to settle both the light and its bringers."

"You fucking bitch—," Val started, but was interrupted by a cuff on the shoulder.

"He asks you nothing," the golden-haired faerie spat. "Say nothing."

"No," said the Lord of the Dark Court. "Let them speak. It is so rare that we guest mortals. I can think of the last time, but then, it was nothing if not memorable." Some of the assembled throng tittered at that, although Val wasn't sure why. "The boy has true Sight, if I'm not mistaken. One of us put out your eye, yes?"

Luis looked around the room, fear etched in his face. He licked blood from his lip and nodded.

"I wonder what you see when you look at me," Roiben said. "But come, tell us what it is you came for. Is it truly in Mabry's possession?"

"She cut out the heart of my—," Val said. "Out of one of the Folk—a troll. I've come to get it back."

Mabry laughed at that, a deep, sensual laugh. Some of the throng laughed, too. "Ravus is long dead by now, rotting in his chambers. Surely you know that. What good is his heart to you?"

"Dead or not," Val said. "I have come for his heart and I will have it."

A wry smile touched Roiben's mouth and Val felt dread creep over her. He looked at Val and Luis

holly black

with pale eyes. "What you ask is not mine to give, but perhaps my servant will be generous."

"I think not," said Mabry. "If you consume the heart of the thing, you consume some of its power. I will relish Ravus's heart." She looked down at first Luis and then Val. "And I will savor it all the more knowing you wanted it."

Val shifted up onto her knees and then stood, wrists still bound behind her back. Blood beat in her ears, so loud it nearly drowned out any other sound. "Fight me for it. I'll wager his heart against mine."

"Mortal hearts are weak. What need have I for such a heart?"

Val took a step toward her. "If I'm so weak, then you must be a real fucking coward not to fight me." She turned to the faeries, to the cat-eyed, those with skin of green and gold, those with bodies stretched too long or too squat or all manner of unnatural proportions. "I'm just a human, aren't I? I'm nothing. Gone in one sigh from one of your mouths, that's what Ravus said. So if you are afraid of me, then you are less than that."

Mabry's eyes glittered dangerously, but her face remained placid. "You have great daring to speak so, here, in my own court, at the steps of my new Lord."

"I dare," Val said. "As much as you dare to act all high and mighty when you're just here to murder him like you murdered Ravus."

Mabry laughed, short and sharp, but there was muttering from some of the assembled Folk.

"Let me guess," Roiben said lazily. "I shouldn't listen to the mortal for one more moment."

Mabry opened her mouth and then closed it again.

"Accept her challenge," said Roiben. "I will not have it said that one of my Court could not best a human child. Nor shall I have it said my murderer was a coward."

"As you wish," said Mabry, turning to Val abruptly. "After I'm done with you, I will put out Luis's other eye and make a new harp from both your bones."

"String me in your harp," Val hissed. "And I'll curse you every time you pluck it."

Roiben stood. "Do you agree to the terms of her challenge?" he queried, and Val suspected that he was giving her a chance to do something, but she didn't know what.

"No," Val said. "I can't bargain for Luis. He's got nothing to do with my challenge."

"I can bargain for myself," Luis said. "I agree to Mabry's terms provided she put up something for

holly black

them. She can have me, but if Val wins, then we go free. We get to walk out of here."

Val glanced at Luis, grateful for his perception and amazed by her own stupidity.

Roiben nodded. "Very well. If the mortal wins, I will give her and her companion safe passage through my lands. And since you have not decided the terms of your combat, I will choose them— you will fight until first blood." He sighed. "Do not think there is any pity in that. Living, should Mabry win your hearts and bones, does not seem so preferable to being safely dead. I, however, have some questions for Mabry that I need her alive to answer. Now, Thistledown, unclasp the mortals and give the girl her arms."

The golden-haired man slid a jagged-toothed key in the locks and the manacles sprang open, dropping to the ground with a hollow sound that echoed through the dome.

Luis stood a moment later, rubbing his wrists.

A woman with chin hair so long that it was woven into tiny braids brought the glass sword to Val and went halfway down on one knee, raising the blade in her palms. Tamson's sword. Val glanced at Mabry, but if she had any reaction to the sight of it, if she even remembered to whom it had once belonged, she gave no sign.

"You can do it," Luis said. "What does she know about fighting? She's no knight. Just don't let her distract you with glamour."

Glamour. Val looked at her backpack, the strap still draped over Luis's shoulder. There was nearly a bottle full of Never there. If glamour was Mabry's weapon, then Val could fight her on those terms. "Give me the bag," Val said.

Luis slid it down his arm and handed it to her.

Val reached in and touched the bottle. Digging down past it, her hand closed on a lighter. It would just take a moment and then Val would be flooded with power.

As she turned, she saw her face reflected in the glass of the blade, saw her own bloodshot eyes and grime-streaked skin before the roving lights under the hill shot the sword through with sudden radiance. Val thought of the girl, Nancy, hit by a train because she was so full of Never that she hadn't seen the gleaming of headlights or heard the scream of brakes. What might Val miss while she was weaving her own illusions? She felt the weight of the knowledge hit her gut like a swallowed stone; she had to do this without any Never singing under her skin.

Val had to fight Mabry with what she knew—years of lacrosse and weeks of the sword, fistfights

holly black

with neighbor kids, who never said she hit like a girl, the ache of pushing her body past what she thought she could endure. Val couldn't fight fire with fire, but she could fight it with ice.

She dropped the lighter and lifted the glass sword from the girl's hands.

I can't fall, she reminded herself, thinking of Ravus and Dave and dominoes all together in neat little rows. *I can't fall and I can't fail.*

The court gentry had cleared away a square path in the middle of the court and Val stepped into it, shrugging off her coat. It puddled on the floor; the cool air prickled the hairs on her arms. She took a deep breath and smelled her own sweat.

Mabry stepped out of the crowd, clad in mist that congealed into the shape of armor. In her hand she held a whip of smoke. The tip dragged tendrils behind it that reminded Val of the way that sparklers burned.

Val took a step forward, parting her legs slightly and keeping them loose at the knees. She thought of the lacrosse field, of the tight-but-loose way to hold the stick. She thought of Ravus's hands, pushing her body into the right formation. Val longed for Never, scorching her from the inside, filling her with fire, but she gritted her teeth and prepared to begin.

Mabry stalked toward the center of the square. Val wanted to ask if they should start now, but Mabry sent her whip whirling and there was no more time for questions. Val parried, trying to slice the whip in half, but it became insubstantial as fog and the blade passed right through.

Mabry shot the whip out again. Val blocked, feigned and thrust, but her reach was too short. She barely staggered out of the way of another blow.

Mabry twirled the whip above her head as if it were a lasso. She smiled at the crowd and the throng of faeries howled. Val wasn't sure if they were showing favor or just crying for blood.

The whip flew out, snaking toward Val. She ducked and rushed in under Mabry's guard, trying one of those fancy moves that looked great if you could manage them. She missed entirely.

Two more parries and Val was tiring fast. She'd been awake for two days and her last meal was a pale faerie apple. Mabry beat her back, so that the Court had to part for Val's stumbling retreat.

"Did you think you were a hero?" Mabry asked, her voice full of mock pity, pitched loud enough for the crowd.

"No," Val said. "I think you're a villain."

holly black

Val bit her lip and concentrated. Mabry's shoulders and wrists weren't moving with the refined control it would take to make the strikes that lanced out at Val. It was her mind that was doing the work. The whip was an illusion. How could Val win, when Mabry could think the whip into changing direction or snaking farther than its length?

Val swung up her sword to block another strike and the misty cord wrapped around the length of the blade. A hard tug jerked it out of Val's hands. The sword flew across the hall, forcing several courtiers to shriek and fall back. As the blade hit the hard-packed earthen floor, it cracked into three pieces.

The whip reached for Val again, flicking out to strike her face. Val ducked and ran toward the remains of the sword, whip whirring just behind her.

"Don't let it bother you that you're about to die," Mabry said with a laugh that invited the other faeries to laugh with her. "Your life was always destined to be so short as to make no difference."

"Shut up!" Val had to concentrate, but she was disoriented, panicked. She was fighting all wrong; she was fighting as if she wanted to kill Mabry, but all she had to do to win was hit her once and all she had to do to lose was to get hit.

Mabry was vain; that much was obvious. She looked cool and she fought cool. Even though she was leaning heavily on her glamour, she was doing it in such a way that made her seem like the better combatant. If she could make the whip grab the blade of the sword, couldn't she just have made it strike Val's hand? Couldn't she conjure knives at Val's neck?

She must want a dramatic triumph. A small scar on Val's cheek. A long laceration across her back. The cord wrapping around Val's neck. It was a performance, after all. The performance of a master performer before a court about to pass judgment on her.

Val stopped, standing just a foot from the hilt of the glass sword, the tang unmarred and part of the blade still attached. She turned.

Mabry was striding toward her, lips curling back into a smile.

Val had to do something unexpected, so she did. She continued just to stand there.

Mabry hesitated only a moment before she sent the smoke whip slashing toward Val. Val dropped to the ground, rolled and grabbed the hilt of what was left of the glass sword, thrusting it up,

holly black

inelegantly, gracelessly, and completely uncoolly into Mabry's knee.

"Hold," cried the golden-haired faerie.

Val dropped the hilt, smeared with just a little blood. It was enough. Her hands started to shake.

Mabry's smoke armor and arms faded away and she was in her gown again. "It matters little," she said. "Your gory memento will rot as your love rots. You will find a corpse no fit companion."

Val couldn't help the smile that spread on her face, a smile so wide it hurt. "Ravus isn't dead," she said, enjoying the blank look that came over Mabry's features. "I pulled down all the curtains and turned him to stone. He's going to be *fine*."

"You couldn't—" Mabry reached out her hand and smoke coalesced into a scimitar. She swept it jaggedly forward. Val stumbled back, turning her head away from the strike. The blade grazed her cheek, tracing a burning line across the skin.

"I said hold," the golden-haired faerie shouted, lifting up the silver box.

"Stop," said the King of the Unseelie Court. "Thrice you have displeased me, Mabry, spy or not. Because of your carelessness, mortals have let daylight into the Night Court. Because of your lack of valor, a mortal won a boon from us. And because of your pettiness, my promise that the mortals would not be harmed in my lands is dishonored. Henceforth, you are banished."

Mabry shrieked, an inhuman noise that sounded like rushing wind. "You dare banish me? I, Lady Nicnevin's trusted spy in the Seelie Court? I, who am a true servant of the Unseelie Court and not a pretender to its throne?" Her fingers became knives and her face pulled unnaturally long and monstrous. She lunged at Roiben.

Val's body moved automatically, the moves she had practiced a hundred, hundred times in the dusty bridge as unconscious as a smile. She knocked aside Mabry's strike and stabbed her in the neck.

Blood spilled down her red dress, spattered Val. The knife fingers clutched Val, opening long wounds in her back as Mabry drew her close, pushing them together like lovers. Val screamed, pain throbbing, cold shock creeping up to paralyze her. Then abruptly, Mabry fell, blood blackening the earthen floor, hands slipping down Val's back. She did not move again.

A wave of noise came from the gentry. Luis rushed forward, pushing aside the faeries in his way to grab Val as she swayed forward.

All Val saw was the glass sword, shattered into jagged pieces, and covered with blood. "Don't fall," she reminded herself, but the words didn't

holly black

seem to be in context any longer. Her vision swam.

"Give me the heart," Luis shouted, but in the chaos, no one heeded him.

"Enough," someone—probably Roiben—said. Val couldn't concentrate. Luis was speaking and then they were moving, pushing through the blur of bodies. Val stumbled along, Luis holding her up, as they turned through corridors underground. The noise of the Court faded away as they made their way out onto the cold hill.

"My coat," Val mumbled, but Luis didn't stop. He steered her into the car and leaned her against it as he pushed back the passenger seat. "Get in and lie down on your stomach. You're going into shock."

There was something about a box. A box with a heart inside, just like in Snow White. "Did you get it from the woodsman?" Val asked. "He tricked the evil queen. Maybe he tricked us, too."

Luis took a ragged breath and let it out in a rush. "I'm taking you to the hospital."

That cut through her haze enough to fill her with panic. "No! Ravus and Dave are waiting for us. We have to go play dominoes."

"You're scaring the shit out of me, Val," Luis said. "Come on, lie down and we'll go to the city.

But don't you go to sleep on me. You stay the fuck awake."

Val climbed into the car, pressing her face into the leather of the seat. She felt Luis's coat settle over her and she flinched. Her back felt as if it was on fire.

"I did it," she whispered to herself as Luis turned the key in the ignition and pulled out onto the street. "I finished the level."

Chapter 14

All human beings should try and learn before they die
what they are running from, and to, and why.

—JAMES THURBER

They arrived in the city as the sun dropped behind them. The drive had been slow. Congested traffic and long lines at the tolls had made the trip stretch longer and Val shifted constantly in the backseat. The icy air from windows Luis refused to close froze her and the pain when the upholstery touched her back made it impossible to turn over.

"You still okay back there?" Luis called.

"I'm awake," Val said, kneeling up and holding on to the passenger side headrest, ignoring how light-headed she felt once she was upright. The silver box sat in the center of the front seat, the dim outside lights highlighting the sculptural wreath of brambles that surrounded a single rose on the surface. "It's already dark."

"We can't go any faster. Traffic is crazy, even in this direction."

She looked at Luis and it felt as if she were seeing him for the first time. His face was bleeding and his braids were loose, hairs frizzing out in a nimbus around his head, but his expression was calm, even kind.

"We'll get there in time," she said, trying to sound brave and sure.

"I know we will," Luis replied, and Val was glad of the human comfort of lies as they continued to weave through traffic.

They pulled up half on the sidewalk of the underpass. Luis turned off the car and jumped out, pushing down the seat so Val could get out too. She grabbed the box and slid from the car as Luis pounded on the wooden tree stump.

Val ran up the stairs, holding the box to her chest. She was already crying as she walked into the dark room.

Ravus lay in the middle of the floor, no longer stone, his skin as pale as marble. Val sank to her knees beside him, opening the silver box and taking out her gory treasure. It was cold and slippery in her fingers as she placed it into the wet, gaping

holly black

wound in his chest. The blood on the floor had dried in black streaks that flaked where she'd stepped and her stomach churned at the sight of it.

She looked up at Luis and he must have seen something in her face, because he kicked over a stack of books, setting dust swirling through the air. Neither of them said anything as the moments slid by, each one meaningless now that they were too late.

Her tears dried on her cheeks and no more came. She thought that she should scream or sob, but neither of those things seemed to express the growing emptiness inside of her.

Val leaned down, letting her fingers slide through Ravus's soft hair, pushing stray locks back from his face. He must have woken when he turned back from stone, woken to an empty chamber and terrible pain. Had he called out for her? Cursed her when he realized that she'd left him to die alone?

Bending low and ignoring the smell of blood, she pressed her mouth to his. His lips were soft and not as cold as she feared.

He coughed and she pulled back, falling into a sitting position. Skin was growing over his chest and his heart was beating in a steady staccato.

"Ravus?" Val whispered.

He opened his golden eyes.

"I hurt everywhere." He laughed and then started to choke. "I can only surmise that's good."

Val nodded, the muscles of her face hurting as they tried to smile.

Luis crossed the room to kneel down on Ravus's other side.

Ravus looked up at him and then back to Val. "You both . . . you both saved me?"

"Come on," said Luis. "You make it sound like it was hard for Val to go to the Unseelie Court, strike a deal with Roiben, challenge Mabry to a duel, win back your heart, and then get back here during rush hour."

Val laughed, but her laugh sounded too loud and too brittle, even to her own ears. Ravus's gaze settled on Val and she wondered if he hated that it was she who'd saved him, if he felt that he would now be indebted to someone who disgusted him.

Ravus groaned and started to sit up, but his strength seemed to fail him and he fell back. "I am a fool," he said.

"Stay where you are." Val scuttled over to a blanket and pushed it under Ravus's head. "Rest."

"I'll be all right," he said.

"Really?" Val asked.

"Really." He reached up to squeeze her shoulder, but she flinched as his fingers grazed over the cuts on her back. His eyes held hers for a long moment, then he pulled a wad of the material of her shirt up. Even out of the corner of her eye, she could see it was stiff with blood. "Turn around."

She did, kneeling up and lifting the back of her T-shirt over her head. She held that pose for a moment, then dropped her shirt back to cover her. "Is it bad?"

"Luis," Ravus said, his voice sharp. "Bring me some things from the table."

Luis collected the ingredients and set them on the floor beside Ravus. First Ravus showed Luis how to salve and treat Val's back, then how to doctor his own ripped piercings, and finally he wove together amaranth, crusts of salt, and long stalks of green grass. He handed them to Luis. "Tie that into the shape of a crown and place it on David's brow. I only hope it will be enough."

"Take the car," Val said. "Come back for me when you can."

"Right," Luis nodded, moving to stand. "I'll bring Ruth."

Ravus touched Luis's arm and he paused. "I was thinking about what was said and unsaid. If rumors from either Court implicate your brother, he will be in great danger."

Luis stood up, gazing out the windows at the glittering city. "I'll just have to think of something. I'll make some kind of bargain. I've protected my brother so far; I'll keep protecting him." He looked at Ravus. "Will you tell anyone?"

"You have my silence," Ravus said.

"I'll try to make sure I deserve it." Luis shook his head as he walked through the plastic curtain.

Val watched him go. "What do you think will happen to Dave?" she asked, her voice low.

"I don't know," Ravus said equally quietly. "But I confess that I care much more about what will happen to Luis." He turned to her. "Or you. You know, you look terrible."

She smiled, but her smile faded a moment later. "I am terrible."

"I know that I have behaved badly toward you." He looked to one side, at the planks of the floor and his own dried blood, and Val thought how strange it was that sometimes he seemed ages and ages older than she, but at other times, he didn't seem any older at all. "What Mabry told me hurt more than I expected. It was easy for me to believe that your kisses were false."

"You didn't think I really liked you?" Val

holly black

asked, surprised. "Do you think I really like you now?"

He turned toward her, uncertainty in his face. "You did go to quite a lot of effort to be having this conversation, but . . . I don't want to read too much of what I hope into that."

Val stretched out beside him, resting her head in the crook of his arm. "What do you hope?"

He pulled her close, hands careful not to touch her wounds as they wrapped around her. "I hope that you feel for me as I do for you," he said, his voice like a sigh against her throat.

"And how is that?" she asked, her lips so close to his jaw that she could taste the salt of his skin when she moved them.

"You carried my heart in your hands tonight," he said. "But I have felt as if you carried it long before that."

She smiled and let her eyes drift closed. They lay there together, under the bridge, city lights burning outside the windows like a sky full of falling stars, as they slid off into sleep.

A note arrived in the beak of a black bird with wings that glistened purple and blue, as though it were made of pooling oil. It danced on Val's window-sill, tapping at the glass with its feet, eyes shining

• • •

That night, on her way out the door, she passed her mom, sitting in front of the television, where a woman's lip was being injected with collagen.

For a moment, the sight of the needle made Val's muscles clench, her nose scent for the familiar burning sugar smell, and her veins twist like worms in her arms, but it was accompanied by a visceral disgust just as strong as the craving.

"I'm going for a walk," she said. "I'll be back later."

Val's mother turned, her face full of panic.

"It's just a walk," Val said, but that didn't settle the unasked and unanswered questions that lay between them. Her mother seemed to want to pretend the last month hadn't happened. She referred to it only vaguely, saying, "When you were away," or "When you weren't here." Behind those words seemed to be vast, black oceans of fear, and Val didn't know how to navigate them.

"Don't be too late," her mother said faintly.

The first snow had fallen, encasing the branches in sleeves of ice and turning the sky bright as day. Val picked her way to the school playground as flurries started up again.

Ravus was there, a black shape sitting on a swing that was too small for him, hunching forward

holly black

to avoid the chains. He wore a glamour that made his teeth less prominent, his skin less green, but mostly he just looked like himself in a long, black coat, gloved hands holding a gleaming sword across his lap.

Val walked closer, sticking her hands in her pockets, finding herself suddenly shy. "Hey."

"I thought you should have one of your own," Ravus said.

Val reached out and ran a finger down the dull metal. It was thin, the crossguard in the shape of braided ivy and the hilt unwrapped by leather or cloth.

"It's beautiful," Val said.

"It's iron," he said. "Crafted by human hands. No faerie will ever be able to use it against you. Not even me."

Val took the blade and sat in the swing beside his, letting her feet drag through the snow, making it into muddy slush. "That's some present."

He smiled, seemingly pleased.

"I hope you'll keep teaching me how to use it."

His smile widened. "Of course I will. You have only to tell me when."

"I was looking at NYU—Ruth likes their film department and they have a fencing team. I know that's a different thing than the kind of fighting you've been teaching me, but I don't know, I was thinking it might not be completely different. And there's always lacrosse."

"You would come to New York?"

"Sure." Val looked back at her slushy feet. "I have some school to finish. I got all your messages." She could feel that her cheeks were hot and blamed the cold. "I was wondering if there was a way to send something back to you."

"Do you mind birds?"

"No. The crow you sent was beautiful, although I don't think he liked me."

"I will have my next messenger await your response."

Just a short time ago, she might have been that messenger. "Have you heard anything about Mabry? What is everyone saying?"

"Rumors from the Courts hold that Mabry was some kind of double agent, but each Court denies her. The exiles in the city know she was the poisoner—the Bright Court appears to be claiming that she was killing at the behest of the Night Court—but so far she has not been linked with Dave. Regrettably, I fear time will reveal his involvement."

"And then?"

"We Folk are a fickle, capricious people. Whim

holly black

will decide his fate, not some mortal idea of jus-
tice."

"So are you going to return to the Bright
Court? I mean, now that you know the truth
about Tamson there's no reason to stay exiled."

Ravus shook his head. "There is nothing for me
there. Silarial counts deaths too lightly." He
reached out a gloved hand and stilled her swing. "I
would remain nearer you for what time there is."

"Gone in one faerie sigh," she quoted.

Leather-clad fingers brushed over her short
hair, rested on her cheek. "I can hold my breath."

Acknowledgments

I am abjectly grateful to have had the Nameless workshop of Philadelphia (Ann, Gail, Judith, Ricardo, Vicky, Ef, Greg) for getting me off to a great start, and the Massachusetts All-Stars (Ellen, Delia, Kelly, Gavin, Dora, Sarah) for getting me through the finish line. When I had no confidence in myself, their confidence in me was invaluable.

There were a lot of people who looked at this book at different stages and offered words of encouragement and advice. I thank you all, but I have to especially thank Phil, Angela, Jenni, and Elka for saying the exact right thing at the exact right time.

Thanks to my tireless editor, Kevin, and my inexhaustible agent, Barry, for believing that I could pull the rabbit out of the hat one more time (and for ignoring all the times I pulled out something entirely different).

Most of all I have to thank Steve, Josh, and Cassie for suffering through the endless writing and rewriting with me, and I have to thank Theo for suffering *me* through the endless writing and rewriting.

holly black